SPEED RAIL

A SINGLE DAD ROMANCE

BRIDGES AND BITTERS
BOOK 3

LAINEY DAVIS

Speed Rail: A Single Dad Romance

By Lainey Davis
Join my newsletter and never miss a new release!
laineydavis.com
© 2023 Lainey Davis

Many thanks to Arwen Davis, Melissa Wiesner and Elizabeth Perry for editorial input.
Edited by The Meet Cute Editor, LLC
Cover by Creme Fraiche Design

Thank you for supporting
independent authors!

 Formatted with Vellum

CONTENT NOTE

This book discusses abortion and death due to complications from pregnancy. I know reading this story might be difficult for some.

Since June 24, 2022, many Americans no longer have the choice whether to continue with a pregnancy. The characters in my book are fictional, but the scenarios and stakes they face are very real in states where the right to bodily autonomy has been revoked.

It is important to me to tell these stories.

1

CASH

I'M UP, I'M UP. SERIOUSLY, I'M UP. IF I KEEP TELLING MYSELF this lie it'll eventually feel true, right? My five o'clock alarm feels cruel this time of year, when the days are getting shorter and the sun is rising a hell of a lot later.

I drag my hands down my face and sit up, fumbling with my phone as I scramble to turn off the alarm before it wakes my daughter. The only thing worse than getting up this early to work on my side hustle would be to get up this early and *not* be able to work on my side hustle because Ruby needs my full attention.

I walk to the door gingerly, sending up silent praise that the floorboards don't creak under my weight. I'm pretty religious about oiling the door hinges and checking the knobs for squeaks, but there never seems to be much I can do about 90-year-old pine boards groaning as I try to sneak out across the back yard to my garage, which I have converted to a makeshift studio.

I grab myself a glass of water and a green apple as I slip out the back door. I figure the walk in the freezing air will stand in for any stretches I should probably do, and I recite tongue twisters as I hurry along, to warm up my voice. It sounds a lot like I'm imitating the neighbor's cat, but it works.

I know voice acting is a dumb pipe dream for a guy like me, but I've been getting some steady work lately recording lectures for a local university and it's nice money. I fell into the work accidentally when one of my clients heard me talking to myself as I installed her ceiling fan. Who knew she'd be looking for someone to record her research? Ask me anything about Appalachian literature. I'm practically an expert.

I leave the garage door unlocked in case Ruby has an emergency. She knows where to find me in the mornings. I usually get 45 minutes to record before she's up and our day runs away from us. I fling open the curtain on my little booth—not much more than a hula hoop with blankets and a music stand with my monitor on it. It looks like a camping shower from the outside...and I guess I did use the same supplies to rig it up. I suspended my mic from the ceiling instead of a hose, and it feels a little bit like an echo of my former life. Back when I had access to real equipment and studio space.

Before.

I finish up gargling and shout a few times before I pull up my work from where I left off yesterday. I pop my lips a few times, take a deep breath, and...I jump because I hear a huge clatter from outside.

I sigh, assuming it's the neighborhood raccoon on a bender in the alley behind the garage. Ruby and I have an end townhouse near the park, so we get more critters than the folks at the other end of the street.

I can edit out a few little bangs in the background if he drops another trashcan lid. But the clanging continues, rhythmically, and I'm suddenly gritting my teeth against pounding rock music.

"What the actual...farts!" I have to stay strong when it comes to 'red words' or Ruby will start repeating them at school again. I can't handle another conversation with her principal about profanity, but I'll admit it's been difficult curbing my instinct to cuss all the time.

I yank open the curtain on my sound booth as the music swells even louder. Nobody on this street would be blasting music like this before dawn. It's mostly retired people and a few families. Even if they're up, they're more likely to listen to the morning news or similar shit. "Shiz," I correct myself out loud, flinging up my garage door.

I squint in the bright light pouring from the warehouse across the alley. I don't know who thought it was a good idea to build a residential neighborhood so close to an industrial warehouse, but here we are. I remind myself how inexpensive my house was back when the warehouse was vacant.

Recently, the owner divided the building into little storage units and workshops for small businesses to rent, but it's mostly people who make small batches of ice cream or robot vacuum prototypes. I barely noticed anyone was there.

I hold a hand up to block the glare and, squinting through the foggy cacophony, I see a woman hurling barbells at the pavement in the alley.

I take a step closer, wondering if I didn't actually wake up with my alarm. Maybe this is a dream I'm having as Ruby pounds on my chest or something. But no. There's a white woman with long brown hair, standing in the cold in a sports bra and leggings, thrusting a barbell over her head and then slamming it into the ground before she squats and picks it up all over again.

A small crowd of other women stands around her, watching intently, all of them swaying to the music. Is this a class?

I take another step closer, definitely not looking at the woman's cleavage as she hoists the weights again. I also do not look at her stomach as she pauses for a breath with her arms over her head before letting the weight drop.

"Woo," she says in a high-pitched voice that carries above the music, dusting off her hands as the other women applaud. "See? You can work up to that. We can—"

She stops when I take another step forward. I stand in the halo of light pouring from the end unit of the building —a space that was up until this moment quiet storage for custom rain barrels.

I cross my arms and raise my brows and wait for someone to turn down the music so we can discuss this situation like rational humans.

The cult leader tosses her ponytail back over her shoulder and adjusts her shoulders. "Welcome to Pipe Fitters," she shouts, smiling at me.

I recoil. I know the guys in the pipefitters union. They are not up before dawn trying to crack asphalt with metal barbells. They're already out on the job cracking concrete with tools. I take a step toward her part of the warehouse and identify the source of the sound: a speaker flashing disco lights to the beat of the music blaring out of it. I bend over, jab at the power button and turn around to see the women have all followed me inside.

The space is no longer filled with rain barrels. There are duct-taped weight benches and old tires and it looks like someone hung ropes from the ceiling. I tilt my head to look for the support joists and frown at the rusty light fixtures.

"Can I help you?" The bra-woman seems affronted, as if

I somehow ruined *her* morning and not the other way around.

"You already ruined my day. Try to follow the noise ordinance from now on." I spin on my heel and stomp back to my own garage, refusing to look at this nuisance as she bends over to adjust the music, turning it back on at a more reasonable volume. Too late to do me any good, because as I roll my own garage door shut, I hear Ruby patter into the room.

"Can I have some of your coffee, Cash?"

She looks up at me hopefully as I shake my head. "We talked about this, Rubes. You're supposed to call me Dad." I pull her in for a side hug and kiss the top of her head. I don't actually mind that she uses my first name. We are a team, after all.

"I'd remember that if I had some coffee." She reaches for my hand and I squeeze her cold fingers as we walk back toward the house we've shared since she was a baby.

I ruffle her hair with my other hand. "I'll pour a splash of it in your milk. But no sugar."

She squeaks, happy with this news. By the time we sit at the table with our morning drinks and I look out the back window, the door is shut across the alley and all the sound is gone. It's possible I imagined the entire thing.

2

PIPER

WELL THAT WAS UNEXPECTED. AS I WATCH THE BEEFY neighbor—a tall, white dude with bright red hair— stomp back into his garage, I try not to think about all the other men in my life who have tried to interfere with my business. That's what brought me here, to this alley with my small following of moms looking for welcoming fitness classes.

I shake my shoulders and smile at the gals. "I guess he didn't like our music." I smile and they titter with polite laughter. "Anyway," I continue, pointing to the weights, "what I showed you is the full movement with weights. We are going to start the movement with just a PVC pipe, to make sure you're comfortable and using proper form."

I gesture for everyone to follow me back into my new gym. It's not really a gym yet—still mostly a garage with some equipment in it. But like I told this early crew, Rocky Balboa trained in a barn and he managed to eventually beat the Russian in *Rocky IV.*

The previous tenant left a few things behind when they moved out, and I took advantage of some of the barrels and lightweight tubes. I pass out some of the tubes and show the class how to move their bodies through a deadlift, a high pull, and an overhead thrust. By six o'clock, all of them have the form down pat, even if just those bodyweight movements are a challenge.

"Think of all the good work you did for your bodies this morning." I high five each of them as they gather their things to hurry home before they need to put their children on the bus. "You can practice with a broom at home!"

When I made the abrupt choice to quit my job at the corporate gym and open my own, I hadn't quite built a name for myself with as many young moms as I wanted. My long-term plan was to work my way into a bunch of moms' hearts and eventually bring them with me when I opened my own mom-centric gym.

Moms tend to enroll in the big box gym because it has on-site childcare. I knew that going in and I did my best to snag as many moms as I could in the personal training program there. It was rewarding work while I dreamed of the future, but my abrasive male colleagues on the training staff slowly tried to poach each and every one of my clients away from me.

These dude bros undercut me in any way possible, but even if they had the look of a fitness-obsessed beefcake, they totally lacked compassion for the clients who need to figure out ways to prioritize themselves and their health after motherhood turned their worlds upside-down.

A few weeks ago, after a particularly passionate venting session, my friend Esther convinced me to quit and told me she'd give me seed money for my own gym. So here I am, shivering a little in a shabby old building with a few eager Pipe Fitters.

One of my students lingers as the others file out. She

sighs. "Piper, I just don't know if I'll be able to make class at this time slot consistently."

I flip a five-gallon bucket upside down and pat it for her to sit. I squat on the ground next to her. "Tell me what's going on, Sarah."

She throws her hands out and waves them around. "It's everything all at once. The baby is teething and my three-year-old has a bunch of half days coming up at school. Something about teacher trainings. Getting up and out the door for a five A.M. class just feels impossible."

I nod and adjust my weight, considering. "I hear you. Can we try to brainstorm some solutions?" I don't want to pressure Sarah, but I also cannot afford to lose her tuition fee right now. Plus I really do want to help her figure out a way she can make space for herself. "What if I did like a web-cam thing and you could do the workout along with us at home? I don't think I could make it interactive, but I could make sure you can see and hear me. You could even take your tube home with you to use!"

Sarah bites her lip and silences the phone in her lap that has started to chirp with rapid text messages. "That's probably Brad wondering where I am."

I pat her shoulder. "I know you have a lot of responsibilities at home. I just also know you seem really happy after you've had a good, cleansing sweat." We both stand and I hold out the hollow length of plastic she'd been using this morning. "Take the tube with you and maybe I can email you once I've got a web cam and link and all that?"

Sarah nods. "I think I can try that. Not having the drive on either end of the workout is a little better, right?"

I grin. "Totally better! Look for my email by Wednesday's class." She heads out and I lie down on the cold, dusty floor. I don't have another class until 9:30, when I see some moms after elementary school drop-off. I resist the urge to pick up my phone and call a friend right now, with my heart racing at the thought of how precarious my cash flow is.

I know it's a risk to sign a lease on this commercial space. Grumpy guy from the alley is probably right about noise ordinances. I've been a little rattled at the condition of my space, to be honest. The landlord showed me another unit when Esther and I were looking, since this one was full of rain barrels at the time. My actual space is...a little rustic.

I'm still glad to be here, though. I lost my very last fuck when Ken from the franchise gym worked a newly post-partum client until she vomited. I'll never forget her look of humiliation as he scolded her for lacking a tough mindset.

"God, I hate him." Just thinking of his smug face during our resultant team meeting sends me right back into rage mode. Ken wasn't even reprimanded. The manager just wanted everyone to make sure we understood hygiene protocols for cleanup.

I knew I couldn't continue working for an organization like that, and I know I have the skills to build clients up physically *and* emotionally. I just...don't have any experience running a business. Yet.

Esther also tipped me off about this rental. I met her in this amazing group of women I stumbled upon one day after college. We call our group Foof...Fresh Out Of Fucks. Samantha came up with the name for our crew of entrepreneurs, engineers, and all around bad-ass women. A few times a month, we meet up for drinks in the back room of Esther's bar, Bridges and Bitters and we just...support each other.

Foof encouraged me to jump ship when I told them about the barfing incident, but Esther helped me make it actually happen. She really knows what she's doing. Esther's bar is this amazing space in a really classy neighborhood. She's killing it and I want to be just like her when I grow up. Only with exercise instead of fancy cocktails.

She wouldn't have funded this gym if she didn't believe in it.

I take a deep breath and stand up from the floor. One thing I know about Esther, is she's never sitting still if she's at work. Even when she's talking me through a life crisis, she's always doing some sort of task at the bar.

I decide to follow her lead and head outside with some bright chalk. I don't have a real sign yet, so I figure I'll just draw some arrows and letters in the alley to guide people my way. Just as I'm crouched over and finishing the last S on PIPE FITTERS, I'm startled by a loud honk.

I jump and turn to see the bearded burly man from earlier, glaring at me from inside a truck. I back up against my building and he accelerates, shaking his head as he passes me.

3

CASH

MY WEEK DOES NOT IMPROVE, ALTHOUGH I DON'T HEAR THE loud woman again. I always feel so flustered at school pickups on half-days. Whoever invented half-days for elementary school can choke on my back hair. By the time I get Ruby out the door and handle my first call of the day, I have to haul ass to make it right back home in time to meet her bus.

I never seem to be able to remember all these impacted school days. Calendaring, as the PTA president calls it, is not a regular part of my life.

I know I need to get better at this shit—*shiz!*—but it's hard. Everything changes all the time...when she was a baby in daycare the schedule was exactly the same, day in and day out.

I shake my head. I can't let myself get hung up in that kind of thinking. Gotta keep looking ahead.

Ruby tipped me off to the half-day early enough that I could schedule an afternoon job near the school, so I decided to pick her up at school rather than have her bus home. It's probably a bad idea to bring a seven-year-old along to replace the GFCI outlets in someone's house, but Ruby knows to keep her fingers away from the power source.

I rest against the brick wall outside the school gym, hoping this is the door where they release the kids. Different age kids come out different doors now that everyone has to go through metal detectors and shit. *Shiz.*

I look around the blacktop to see if I recognize any other parents from Ruby's class.

I spot a mom I've seen before. And then I realize I also saw her this morning in my alley. Just great.

She waves and makes her way toward me. "Cash! Hey. Aren't these half-days the worst?" She's got a baby on one hip and a toddler clinging to her ankles. She blows some hair up off her forehead and looks over her shoulder. "I can never remember which door our kids come out..."

I breathe a deep sigh of relief. "Me neither. I think we're both at the right place though." The toddler squats and shoves a piece of gravel in his mouth, and I quickly bend and scoop him up, without thinking. "Hey, man, spit that out." He looks at me, stunned, and starts to cry. I wipe the pebbles off his tongue while his mouth is open to scream.

"Oh my goodness, thank you. He keeps doing that!" Sarah—*that's her name*—tries to reach for the boy while keeping the baby on a hip just as the doors open and a flood of screaming children pours out of the school.

"It's okay, Sarah. Ruby ate rocks until at least kindergarten." Sarah tries to juggle both her kids and I realize I'm definitely not the only one here feeling like I'm in over my head. "Here, let me hold the baby, maybe, and you can help him calm down."

"Are you sure?" She seems uncertain. I don't blame her. There aren't very many men at school pickup. I know how all the stereotypes go. I also know Ruby had no choice in the matter, so I just got good at keeping her alive. Babies usually like me. My mom says it's the red beard. I scoop up this sweaty baby, and she reaches two damp hands right into my mustache. Sarah bounces the toddler and smiles.

We both scan the sea of yelping gremlins for our kids. Sarah looks like she's about to say something to me, and then pauses. "What's up?" I say this around a mouthful of baby fingers.

Sarah shrugs. "You seemed really grouchy this morning with Piper. Do you know her?"

"Piper?" I pretend like I forgot the name of the woman from the alley. The woman with the loud music and crumbling ceilings and a muscled line down the center of her abs that I definitely would never lick.

Sarah sets the toddler down and reaches for her baby. "She's the best fitness instructor I've ever had. She just really gets what it's like for moms to actually make it in person for a workout." Sarah dabs at the baby's face with her own shirt collar and smiles at me. "She's hooking me up with online classes until I get more in the swing of things with the school year."

I'm about to tell Sarah there's no way Piper has adequate internet service in that concrete warehouse. I can't even make a cell phone call from my neighborhood half the time. But it doesn't matter because both our kids crash into us at the same time and small talk flies out the window.

"Cash!" Ruby punches me in the hip. "I got an 18 on my spelling test."

"Hey, Dad," I mumble, waving at Sarah and her son as Ruby runs off toward my truck. I hardly fit in the back seat to help her with her booster seat, so I stand on the curb and try talking her through buckling herself properly. "Is 18 a good score or a bad one? Here, honey, you have to let the belt go all the way back in when it's stuck like that. Try again."

"Eighteen is terrific. I get to move up to the green spelling list." She clicks the buckle into place and I nod, closing the door and tossing her backpack up front with my stuff.

"And I take it green is also a good thing?" I pull out from the curb slowly, making sure to avoid darting children and flustered parents. I think of Ruby's maternal grandparents begging me to move near them, where the schools have parking lots and pickup lanes and crossing guards.

I look back at my daughter, who is thriving in the city public schools despite the frantic pickup procedures. She rattles off her new spelling words to me from memory— button, mitten, kitten. How could I ever move her to a state where her rights are limited? A state where her mother died bringing her into this world?

I tug a hand through my beard, feeling a little crust where the baby drool is hardening. "Hey, Rubes, you good to come with me on a job this afternoon? Hold my tool belt while I fix some outlets?"

"Sure, Cash. How do you spell cotton? Is that one with an -en?"

"They do all sound similar, huh? You know I used to have a teacher who made us pronounce things very, very slowly and use all the different parts of our mouths."

"A teacher at electronic school?"

"Electrician, Rubes. And no. This was when I was in college. When I met your mom."

"Show me the mouth tricks."

I pull over in front of the house for my next job and turn around in my seat, smiling. I haven't thought of these specific vocal exercises in a long time. Ruby laughs as I open my mouth wide, stretching my cheeks and flicking my tongue as I say COTTON very slowly, much deeper than my usual register.

She claps her hands. "Do it again."

I grin. "Let's do it together."

4

PIPER

A CHUNK OF THE CEILING FELL DOWN IN MY GYM TODAY. I'M kind of a mess about it.

I feel like such a failure calling Esther all the time, but I'm honestly in way over my head here. She insists she can spare the money and just wants my business to exist, but I can't help feeling like...a mess.

I park sort of illegally in the alley near my new building and bite my lip, waiting to see if she can take my call right now.

I lock the doors to my car and make my way into the new Pipe Fitters HQ. I know the name is kind of cheesy, but I want to lean in to my Pittsburgh union roots—my dad has been a card carrying member of the pipe fitters and boiler-makers union for decades. Plus the name is cute. It just is.

"What's new, Pipes?" Esther doesn't sound annoyed at all. I release a breath. I'm not sure why I worried she would be—she's never been annoyed by any of our friends.

I nod as I shove open the door to the gym and tell Esther that I think I need a building inspection. "Are there check-lists or something? You know I just signed this lease kind of on a whim and now here I am with a few clients and a dream."

"Have you gone to the small business resource center at the library downtown?" I hear the clinking of glassware in the background. As per usual, Esther is in motion, doing all the small tasks nobody sees but everyone feels the minute they step into her bar.

"I didn't know the library had business resources..."

"Oh, the library has everything. Hell, the one in Millvale rents out tools, Piper. You need a hoe?"

I laugh, feeling some of the tension ease. Like somehow this small bit of guidance will help me feel more secure in my plans. "I don't need garden tools but I might actually need tools to assemble all the gear I've got on order."

"Are you making any structural changes to your space? I'd deal with permits before equipment if you're doing any construction."

"Hmm." I look around the garage. I mean, it really is a garage, just walls and a rolling door. I don't even have a bathroom in here. The landlord said the tenants have access to the bathrooms inside the larger building. It would be nice to have a water fountain at least. "Do I need fire sprinklers or whatever?"

Esther grunts. Maybe she's changing out a keg. "You'll have to ask the library folks that. I have sprinklers, but I have more people here more frequently than you. Also I own my building."

"Ugh, why is all this so hard?"

"What would Sam or Nicole say to that question?"

We both robotically repeat *If it were easy, everyone would do it.* And then we share a laugh. I hear Esther pause whatever she was doing and she says, "Piper, you jumped in the deep end, but honestly those assholes gave you a shove. Go to the library, get organized, and maybe have your classes meet in the park or something until you figure out what you need in the building space."

"The park? Can I just show up there with paying clients and lead a workout?" I feel the need to emphasize paying clients. Esther didn't put a time limit on the loan she gave me and I don't even think she wants interest, but I still want her to believe I'm going to make it.

"It's a public space, Pipes. You can do pretty much anything in the park. Did Chloe tell you she walked up on people doing it in Frick Park the other day?"

"No! In the city park? Were they naked?" It must have thrilled our friend Chloe to come upon that little tryst. She's a steamy romance writer, although her books are all set in the 1700s.

"She said partially. I bet she chased them away trying to ask questions."

"Ha! Imagine?" I imitate Chloe's voice, saying, "Excuse me, can I just ask you about your experience?"

Esther and I laugh a little more about the park people and she gets off the line to start opening for the day. I decide to sit on a tire and map out some lesson plans. There's a park a block from here that would work for my classes while it's light outside. I still don't have a good solution for my five o'clock mamas, though.

It's so important to me to build my schedule around my core clientele. These moms do so much for their families and put themselves last. I saw it in my own mom and, well, if I can prevent even one family from losing their mom too early by helping her stay healthy, then I'll do whatever it takes.

A loud honk startles me from my lesson plans and I jump to my feet. I peek out the door to the gym and see the grumpy man in his monster truck. Who drives a truck like that in the city? He's laying on the horn pretty aggressively and I stick my head into the alley.

I realize I must be blocking his garage. "One second," I shout, running back into the gym to grab my keys. I fumble around with the lanyard, because I always feel flustered when I know someone is irritated with me.

When I get outside I see that he's blocked my car with his truck and he's leaning against the door, his arms crossed and his expression hard. "I could have you towed," he growls.

"I said I was coming to move it. I'm sorry I blocked your garage." I move to open the car door but I realize I'm not going to be able to do anything because there's a car directly behind me and he's got his truck parked diagonal in the alley.

"Are you going to move so I can move?" I raise my brows expectantly and tap my foot. I watch him watch my shoe.

"I haven't decided yet."

"Okay, that's weird. You either want me to move or you don't, but please decide because I have things to do. Some of us are working right now." I wince inwardly. I have no idea if he's been at work all day or what. That last line was straight from my dad.

The grumpy guy shakes his head. I try not to notice the gold streaks in his red hair and I try really hard not to think about running my hands through all that thick, wavy wonder. He's so big and mean and I'm not sure why, but I feel my tummy flipping a little at the thought of wrestling around with him.

"I ought to just back up over that toy car to spite you."

"Go for it, Sasquatch. I know people at the DMV."

"Sasquatch?" I watch as he bites back a laugh. His

expression softens and he shakes his head. "Don't block my spot again."

He climbs in his truck and drives off. I stare after him for a bit and then I hear the telltale sound of more debris skittering down from my ceiling. I decide to head home and finish my planning there.

5

CASH

I HAVE NO REASON FOR HAVING SUCH A SHORT FUSE WITH THIS woman. What the heck is wrong with me? I just tore around the block like a jagoff, revving the engine on my work truck like I don't live in a quiet neighborhood. I hardly ever park behind my garage anyway, but there was a moving van in my regular spot when I got home with Ruby.

I saw the van was gone and thought I could rush outside real quick to move my truck, but nope. I have to instigate a cranky stand-off with the loud lady. Now I'm even more stressed. I ease the truck into the space in front of my house and I see Ruby dancing around in the picture window. I guess she's over me yelling at her for knocking shit over at my client's house. This afternoon has been a nightmare. I absolutely hate yelling at my kid. That's not the kind of parent I want to be. I need to apologize for snapping at her.

Ruby's usually so careful and I really think she was trying her best to help me out but she backed into a teetering pile of books, which crashed into my client's heap of snow globes. The result was me doing the job for free to appease the homeowner and having to personally call the library to explain why the books are all covered in glitter water.

I take a few deep breaths and squeeze the steering wheel as I watch Ruby dance along with those Kid Bop idiots on TV. God, I love my daughter. Despite me being an idiot know-nothing trying to raise her, Ruby seems pretty normal. She's doing okay, which means I just need to stay the course. No more dumb mistakes.

I make my way into the house and sink into the couch as Ruby punches the air in time with the music. "You going to ask me for a silver space suit to go with that routine?" I chuckle, knowing full well we already have a silver space suit somewhere in her dress-up bin.

She pauses and frowns at me. "I can't hear when you talk over the song." I hold my hand up as an apology and watch her dance for a bit longer. With a groan I lean forward and unlace my boots, setting them to the side and wiggling my toes in my socks. They're getting a little threadbare. I guess I'd add shopping to my to-do list if I ever had time to write one.

"Hey, bug, it's Friday. Do you want to go get some pizza?"

Ruby freezes and spins to face me. "Yes! I love that idea. Can we put pineapple on it?"

I shake my head. "Absolutely not. But hey, we need to go to the store first. What kinds of stuff do you need? I need socks." I wave my foot at her and she shrugs. I never can get used to having to know what I need *and* what she needs. I sigh. "Okay, you keep dancing. I'm going to walk around the house and make a list of what we need." I look around the room. "Do we have paper?"

Ruby laughs and points to the dining room table. She's got a school notebook sitting there with about 700 colored pencils. I nod and rip a sheet out of the back of the notebook, finding a pencil that actually has a point on it. It's purple, but it'll do for a shopping list.

I start with the kitchen since I know we need groceries. I'm about halfway through my list of lunch food items when Ruby stomps into the room. "Dad, I want to go to the playground while I wait."

"Oh, I'm 'dad' now?" I raise a brow at her. She nods her head and I smile. "Go on. Look both ways at the stop sign. I'll be there soon." She throws her arms around my leg and runs out the front door, leaving it open behind her.

I stick my head out and watch as she crosses the street. We're starting to get more cars in the neighborhood now that there are businesses moving in to the warehouse. I'm going to have to talk to someone about getting crosswalk lines repainted or something. Ruby's pretty careful about street crossings, but she's no match for distracted drivers on cell phones who are late for their fitness class.

Once Ruby is safely frolicking through the grass, I close the door and finish the grocery list. I take a quick inventory of our cleaning supplies and head upstairs to check through my drawers and see what I need. I remember that my mom said she'd take Ruby shopping for cold-weather clothes this weekend.

Since I had her so young, I don't really know anyone with kids older than her to pass down clothes. I never really stopped to think about how often kids need new pants.

Before Ruby came along, I was too busy pretending an electrician's kid from Pittsburgh would somehow end up on the stage somewhere. My parents' friends were all guys from the trades, whose kids all planned to go into the trades. I don't know how I got the acting bug, but it always made me feel like a weirdo.

And now I'm clipping coupons for bargain underpants

and watching for shoe sales, because I swear my daughter goes through ten pairs of sneakers a year.

I change into jeans and an old t-shirt and stuff my list in my back pocket. I cram a Pittsburgh baseball hat on my head and make my way to the park to find Ruby. When I get outside I see my daughter halfway up an oak tree, staring at a group of women doing jumping jacks in the grass.

"That's new," I mutter. We don't usually get people exercising in Westinghouse Park. Hell, it took years to get the city to resurface the playground here and we don't even have bathrooms in our park.

But, as I get closer to the scene, I see that of course it's Piper leading the activities. I hear her chipper voice encouraging the women as they squat down and jump into the air. Ruby shimmies down the tree and starts to move along with them. Piper smiles at her and I stiffen. There's no way I want my kid interacting with the neighborhood menace.

Thankfully Ruby turns my way after a few jumps and I beckon for her to come to me. She waves at the women and runs toward me. I snag her hand and turn quickly toward home. "Come on, kiddo. Let's get shopping."

"Don't forget the reusable bags, Cash."

I open the door to our car and point to the canvas bags that live on the front passenger seat. "I thought I got to be dad again?"

Ruby shrugs and shoves me away as I lean in to buckle her in the booster seat. "I can do it myself."

"Oh yeah? Let me see." I keep waiting for her to be tall enough that we can get rid of this thing, but I guess if she really can do all the steps herself it's not so bad.

"I got it in the truck, remember?"

I nod and then smile as I hear the buckle click into place. "Wow. We should celebrate with pizza."

She settles in to the seat. "Pineapple on my half."

I walk around the car to my side and look at her in the rearview mirror as I get myself situated. "How did you get so gross?"

Ruby burps at me in response and I laugh as I back out of our parking spot. I crank on the radio and the two of us sing along to Neil Young. I remind myself that even though my day was pretty crappy, I have a daughter interested in great music. And that's pretty cool.

6

PIPER

"Sarah, can you see me?" I wave my hand in front of the laptop screen. I check my phone and she texts me back a thumbs up. "Awesome!" I turn to the rest of the workout group who is here in person. "Okay, I know some of you heard I'm doing park workouts with the after-school crowd, but we're not supposed to be over there until it's light out. Plus that's maybe not safe."

The moms murmur their agreement. I gesture around the room, praying nothing else falls from the ceiling today. I shimmied up and down my climbing ropes a few times and everything seemed secure. "Everyone grab your tube from last week and spread out so you have lots of space. We're going to warm up by going through our form and then I think today we will add a bit of speed."

"Good thing I found a new sports bra!" We all laugh as Ayana shimmies her shoulders, her dreads dancing along her back as she moves. My friend Nicole hooked me up with a recommendation for a bra whisperer who carries gear for all cup sizes. My clients have been heading up there in droves to get fitted.

I take everyone through the warmup and the gym starts to feel a little warm. "Now we're talking, ladies. Feel all that heat we're generating? How's everyone doing?"

I roll the garage door up a few feet to let in some fresh air and crank up the tunes as we all pound out some body-weight lunges. "Okay," I shout above Lizzo. "We're going to do some side planks. Remember, these are going to help those ab muscles come back together if they're still separated after pregnancy."

I sing along as I circle the room, correcting people's form and offering some modifications. The women hold the position for nearly a minute before I tell them it's okay to drop and we all end the workout with a chorus of loud whoops.

Immediately afterward, I hear a series of clangs and shouted curses from across the alley. I roll to my side and look out the crack of the open door to see my grouchy neighbor standing outside kicking his trash cans. He's breathing as heavily as the moms who just worked their core to the limit.

He glares at me and then storms back inside his garage.

I make my way to my feet and dust off my backside. "I'll try to get some yoga mats for us to use until I can get the foam flooring put in," I say, turning down the music.

I squat in front of the laptop to check on Sarah. I give a thumbs up and tell her I'm going to end the live stream before turning to the other women in the gym. Ayana leans against the wall, chugging from her water bottle. "Was that Cash Brennan growling at you in the alley?"

"I'm not sure. We weren't formally introduced."

Another student, Naomi, nods her head as she makes her way back up to her feet. "That's Cash. I saw him last time when he was mad about the music. I bet he's worried we'll wake up Ruby."

"Hm." I hadn't considered we'd be in danger of waking anyone up. All the gyms I've worked at before this have been huge and we've blared music at will. But I guess if I'm opening the door then the neighbors can hear. "I'll have to see what I can do about the morning classes. I don't want the neighbors to hate me!" My heart races, thinking about getting shut down and having to wait tables or something so I can pay back Esther. Would she let me work off my debt at her bar?

Ayana pats my arm. "Nobody could hate you, Piper. Except tomorrow when my muscles are screaming. I'll hate you then."

We all laugh, but I place a hand on Ayana's. "You should never be sore to the point of pain. It should be a good hurt, more of a twinge. I don't want anyone to injure themselves."

The class all nods. We've been through this before. Half of them joined me over here because the trainers at the old gym, the ones who poached my clients away, worked them until they were in danger of lactic acid poisoning.

I smile at the class and pick up my laptop. "Okay, who wants to share goals for the week. I've got my list ready." I decided that a key element of Pipe Fitters would include fitness goals, other health goals, and personal goals for each week. "I'll share that my personal goal is to get to the small business center at the library. I have some work to do, as you might have seen!"

Naomi gives me a thumbs up. "You should send an email about what sorts of contractors you need. I'm sure between all of us we know folks who can get you some bargains."

"You are so sweet, Naomi. I'll be sure and do that once I know what I need to fix." I smile at her. "Now what's one of your goals?"

She winces. "Gotta schedule my mammogram."

"Yes! Excellent goal. Who else?" I make notes on people's plans to go for walks with their kids, get their cholesterol checked, and buy themselves new underwear that actually fit. "I love all of these," I say, meaning it. "Look for my email after I make a plan and maybe I'll toss in a bonus workout opportunity for the weekend if anyone is up to a park outing."

I wave as they file out of the gym and up the alley to the street by the park.

7

CASH

I CAN SEE WHY MY DAD LOST HIS HAIR SO YOUNG. I REACH UP to mine and give it a tug to make sure it's still attached to my scalp. The damn workout bunny across the alley ruined my morning recording session. Again.

I know it's not glamorous work I'm doing. Voice acting doesn't put me in front of a live crowd or anything like that. Heck, this latest voiceover gig is for a public service announcement about flu shots. But it's acting work and I love it. I love escaping into that booth and performing a role, even if I'll never see the audience. Even if I'm just telling people to get their kids vaccinated.

I've done laxative ads, too. I'm not particular. Once I got the lecture samples back from that first client, I got a little website set up and started getting regular hits for freelance jobs. It's the one tiny thread I still have connecting me to that life I thought I'd live.

Before...everything.

Not to mention, I do have a deadline and these clients expect me to deliver the work or they're certainly not going to send me any more of it. I have exactly one hour a day to do this when I'm not working or actively parenting my child. And now, apparently, that hour has become a sound check for a really bad pop band, at dangerous decibel levels.

Should I have burst into the alley and made a stink? Definitely not.

I don't have to turn around to know that my clatter with the trash cans woke up my kid. As soon as I get to the back door she's standing there waving an unopened box of cereal at me. "Cash! Can we open the cinnamon squares today? It's not candy. Remember, you checked and there are whole grains."

I roll my eyes. "I don't think you know a whole grain from any other kind of grain."

Ruby scrunches up her face in thought. Eventually I ruffle her hair. "Come on, squirt. Let's dig in."

I promised her mother I'd try my best to be present with Ruby. I expend a lot of effort into leaving my anger out in that alley and greeting my daughter with the best mood I can muster. We share a bowl of cereal in the living room, watching *Garfield* together until it's time for me to nag her to brush her teeth so we can go meet the school bus.

The other bus stop parents are circled up, talking about upcoming vacations and Thanksgiving travel. I never feel like I have anything to offer, and we've all adopted a habit of comfortably ignoring one another.

I lean against the light pole at the corner, looking for the bus and refusing to let my eye drift toward that alley. Toward the woman who has no business walking around with an ass that round while simultaneously destroying my passion project.

I snort at myself for even thinking the phrase 'passion project,' and wave to Ruby as she climbs on the bus. I try to think of what I might do to salvage this PSA. I have day-job appointments booked this morning and every morning until the deadline. I purse my lips, wondering how much my mother would scold me if I asked her to keep an eye on Ruby for me after school.

I don't want to diminish the help my parents gave me when she was first born, but it sure seems like there was a finite amount of support they had the energy to lend out. Mom's already taking her shopping this weekend. I hate to ask for anything extra.

But I don't see any other way around this, so I dial my mother's cell knowing she's probably on the way to the rusty trailer she and Dad use as headquarters for the family electrical business. "Cashel? You're not sick are you?"

"Morning, Mom. No, no, I'm fine. You and Dad doing good?" I can hear her rolling her eyes. She doesn't approve of small talk. I get that from her. "I was actually wondering if I could ask a favor."

She sighs. I wince. "I was hoping Ruby could hang out with you for a little after school today?"

"Cashel. Son. You know it's banjo night."

Every Wednesday for as long as anyone can remember, the Pittsburgh Banjo Club has played at the Elks Lodge on the North Side. You'd think the musicians would all be in their 90s, and many of them seem to be, but there are actually players my age up there, too. My parents haven't missed a show in years.

I always hoped their interest in this form of live music would help them understand my aspirations, but they see a big difference between people playing for fun and people investing in fine arts tuition.

"Sorry, Mom. I forgot what day it was."

"Well, that's because you don't look at a calendar. Never

have been good at that, have you? You and your brother both. Not sure how I went wrong with that…"

"I have other gifts, Mom." I quote my grandmother and hope it'll stir up a soft memory in my mother.

It does the trick because she clucks her tongue and says, "Well, I'm sorry I can't help you out. But Ruby is welcome to stay the night this weekend after we go shopping."

"I'm sure she'd love that, Mom. I'll check in after my 8:30."

We hang up and I spend an uneventful work day fretting about my inability to make things work with my side hustle. I should view this as evidence that that career was never meant to be, but I can't seem to let the dream die. Every day, my electrician work feels like work, and every minute I spend in the recording booth just feels exciting.

Maybe I wasn't cut out for excitement.

WHEN I MEET Ruby's bus after school, I see that she's got pretty calm energy. We go in the house and she walks over to the table to show me her homework packet, like usual. "I bet I can do both the math pages today."

I nod. "I don't doubt it." She gets to work, knowing she's got more Kid Bop music videos in her future if she finishes her work without arguing. "Hey, Rubes, what would you think if I went into the garage to finish up some work while you finish your work? I trust you to wait for the TV until you do both pages."

She shrugs. "That sounds okay."

I feel my stomach lurch with excited potential. Is she finally old enough that I don't need to stay an arm's length away to keep her safe? "You know you can come get me if something happens."

"Like if the remote doesn't work?"

I laugh. "I meant like if you're bleeding, kid."

I hurry out the back door, stretching my jaw on the hop, shaking out my shoulders and trying to remember where I left off the last time I was able to actually record. I struggle the most with the portions where I have to quickly read all the risks and potential adverse reactions to the flu shot, so I cluck my tongue off the roof of my mouth a few times and slip my headphones on.

I fire up my equipment and stand in place, breathing deeply and emitting a few deep groans to prepare. I pull up the script on my screen, open my mouth to begin...and stare in surprise as my daughter yanks open the curtain to my booth.

She has tears in her eyes and her hand is bleeding.

My stomach sinks.

I feel flames of guilt lick up my sides.

"What happened, Ruby?"

I'm by her side in a flash, my work abandoned. Her lip wobbles and she hiccups. "My pencil tip broke and I tried to use the sharpener by the stairs. But it was jammed."

I close my eyes and groan. Our house came with one of those old-fashioned crank pencil sharpeners fastened to the wall and Ruby has been fascinated with it for years. She will spend twenty straight minutes sharpening a brand new pencil all the way down to the eraser just for the fun of it.

"Can I see, sweetheart?" She holds out her finger and I see a few shallow cuts, like she must have been jiggling around the blades to loosen all the shavings. I nod my head and kiss her cheek. "Not so bad. Come on, let's get the bandages."

She whimpers. "Do I need to go to the hospital?"

"No, baby, not for this." I pick her up and carry her into the house, knowing I'll have to email the client and tell them I'll miss this deadline.

I can't finish even a short ad spot. Not at this stage of my life. "We're going to wash it clean and put some cream on it and wrap it up. It'll be like it never happened."

She nuzzles into my chest as I carry her into the kitchen and then I plop her on the counter. "I'm sorry I messed up your homework, Dad."

"Will you write my teacher a note?" I wink at her as I run her fingers under the tap.

"You have a teacher?"

"Nah. I was being silly. Did it work?" I finish dabbing the cream on and stick a beige bandage on before she can pester me about finding one with robots.

Ruby considers her finger and looks up at me. "It wasn't that funny."

"Ah. Well, maybe next time."

She inhales a shaky breath and I can tell she's trying to get past the tears. "Will you sing me a song?"

Who could say no to a question like that? I melt a little inside and pick her up, tucking her head against my chest as I work my way through a Beatles album. She falls asleep in my arms, like she used to as a baby.

ONCE I GET Ruby to bed, I know I should follow. I can't sacrifice sleep to work on my side hustle at night because then I'll be a bitchy dad *and* a bad electrician. Instead I pace the halls upstairs and fret about this predicament.

Things can't go on like this. I'm not asking for much over here.

I simply need the five o'clock hour to be peaceful so I can do my work. We already have laws in place about this. Noise ordinances exist for a reason! I can tell you right now my octogenarian neighbors would be out blowing leaves at four in the morning if we didn't have rules.

Why should Piper get to break them just because her ass looks good in lycra?

Not that she tried to skirt around enforcement with her looks. It's just that...I don't really know whether anyone has dropped by to check in on her business and make sure things are up to code.

I pause my pacing and look out my bedroom window across the back yard, across the alley to the dark row of garage doors on the old warehouse.

I think about the crumbling ceiling I saw in there, about the shoddy wiring I know nobody has bothered to fix in decades.

Rules only work if everyone follows them, right? Something like that?

I did ask her to keep it down back there and she doesn't. She blares the music every damn morning. I could call the cops.

I pull my phone out of my pocket and decide instead to text my buddy Ben who works down at the inspection office.

> Hey, man. Anyone from your group ever come out my way to check on those new businesses going in behind my place? In the warehouse?

I stare at my phone for a few beats, turn it off, and climb into bed.

8

PIPER

ESTHER WRINKLES HER NOSE AT MY CAR AS PER USUAL. SHE wriggles inside and reaches awkwardly for her seatbelt. "You know this is a toy car and not a real vehicle, right?"

"Shows what you know! I bought it at a real car store."

"I believe the preferred term is dealership."

I nudge her with my shoulder, because she's close enough to me for that inside my zippy little Fiat. "Whatevs, Esther. I can park perpendicular to the curb if I need to. And I always get a spot near your bar."

To illustrate my point, I gesture at the front door of Bridges and Bitters, where I picked her up directly outside since she offered to come take a look at Pipe Fitters with me today and debrief what I learned at the library.

We shoot up Penn Avenue without too much traffic mid-morning, and I can weave around giant trucks pretty handily.

Esther stares at me as I cruise through a yellow light. "I half expect the horn to make a meep sound. Like the Roadrunner."

I chuckle and toot the horn as I approach the alley by my business. My very own business. I toot the horn again in celebration. "Okay," I admit. "It's a puny horn. It's got growth potential."

I make sure to park in a real spot this time, not anywhere near the angry lumberjack's garage, and tug Esther's arm to show her my slice of real estate.

"Hm," Esther says, running a hand down the doorjamb. Brick dust coats her finger by the time I unlock the door. "This is definitely a downgrade from what Alessio showed us, Pipes."

"I know it's a work in progress. The other space was, too." I snap the lights on inside and they flicker a little, as per usual, only this time there's a popping sound that scares us and we both jump.

"Was that a spark, Pipes?"

I look up at the industrial metal domes covering the weird light-bulbs on the ceiling. Are they bulbs? I'm not even sure what the right vocabulary word is for those glass things. "Well, that's the first thing the librarians said I should do is get an electrician in here. I just need to find one. Do you have someone?"

Esther shrugs. "I'll look in my book later. The guy I have is pretty old and grouchy, though."

"Oh, grouchy is my new normal here apparently." I point across the alley. "I've already pissed off the nearby home owners."

Esther raises a dark brow and leans against the wall. I don't miss her checking it for stability first. "What did you do?"

I roll my eyes and sigh. "I was playing my music pretty loud. Okay, it was really loud, but you know I'm used to being in the big gyms where that's normal." Esther nods. "And, you know, my classes start at five. In the morning."

Esther winces. "Well maybe that's something to add to the list...volume of inspirational jams." She claps her hands. "Okay, walk me through it. What've you got?"

I nod. "All right. Picture this." I walk over to the far wall where I just finished setting up racks for the dumbbells and kettlebells. "I'm going to paint this wall with inspirational quotes. Not the fake positive toxic bullshit quotes. Actual inspirational stuff." Esther nods. I keep pointing. "I'll have shelves for floor mats and disinfectant spray and rags. Then here I'm going to hang pull-up bars. And these tires were already here when I moved in! I got some sledge hammers and—"

"Piper Conklin?" A white man in a shirt and tie leans his head in the door.

I purse my lips. "Yes. Can I ask who wants to know?" Suddenly I'm very glad Esther is with me, as I wasn't expecting anyone to drop in and I forgot to lock the door behind me when I came in. I'm going to have to work on so many things if I'm going to succeed running this place by myself. I can see why Esther keeps that chrome pipe behind the bar.

The man nods. "I'm Ben Barber from the city office of building inspections." He holds up a badge. Esther beckons for him to come closer so she can actually read it. God, she's so much more savvy than me. Esther nods and gestures for him to continue. "Well, I think I have some bad news for you." Ben looks up at the lights and winces. "I can see right away that there are a number of things not up to code about this establishment."

I look at Esther and back to Ben. "Isn't the owner responsible for that kind of stuff? I'm just a tenant."

Ben nods sympathetically. I choose to think it was a sympathetic nod. "Well, unfortunately the business model with this space places the responsibility for these updates onto the tenants. I met with the owner this morning and reviewed some of the leases." The lights pop again and Ben flicks the switch off. "Ms. Conklin, I'm going to have to close you down until you can fix the electrical and get the all-clear from a structural engineer."

I blink a few times. "Close me down?"

He slaps an orange sticker on the door of my business. My door. The one I just added a sign to. "You cannot have customers or clients in this space until I say so." He hands me a business card and a piece of a triplicate form.

It's got some numbers written on it and Esther huffs. "A fine? You're giving her a fine?"

Ben coughs. "Yes, well, I'm afraid that's standard for operating prior to inspection."

"What proof do you have that she was in operation?" Esther crosses her arms across her chest and raises a dark brow at Ben, who definitely seems as intimidated as I feel whenever Esther kicks into boss mode.

Ben gestures at me and Esther, who snorts. "I'm not a client, asshole. I'm her business partner."

My eyes widen and Esther shakes her head at me as Ben stares at his notes. "Okay. Okay. Well, then you should know the protocol so—"

"So you're going to cancel the fucking fine, asshole. Don't act like your boss hasn't tried to shake me down at Bridges and Bitters."

Ben sighs and plucks the yellow sheet from my fingers, crumpling it. "I'll look for a call from you both. Our office can send a recommended list of contractors if you—"

"We'll find our own vendors, thank you." Esther pushes him toward the door and closes it in his face before he can say another word and, thankfully, before I pass out from hyperventilating.

9

CASH

I come out of my last appointment of the day to a text from Ben.

> You owe me a beer, jagoff.

I frown at the phone and send him a few question marks. It rings in my hand and I click accept before Ben starts bellowing in my ear. "You didn't tell me you were sending me into a Siren's lair. Gawd almighty, what a morning."

"You paid a call on the loud woman behind my house, then?"

"I don't know about loud, but her friend sure is full of hellfire. I swear she was trying to burn the flesh off my bones with her glare."

I try to think what friend Ben could be referring to. I've only ever seen mom-type women back there with Piper, and while they're all fierce in their own way I doubt they would accost a city building inspector. "Not sure what that's about.

But I actually can go out this weekend if you want to grab a drink. My mom is keeping Ruby overnight."

I wince. I try not to bring up my kid when I'm talking to my friends without kids. I don't want to be that guy. Some of them are in a place now where they're starting to think about starting a family, but they sure weren't when we were 18 and I got Heather pregnant our first semester of college.

"Oh, yeah? I haven't seen you out in an age, man."

"Yeah. Been awhile. But who was mean to you? Did you fine her for disorderly conduct?"

"I'm not a cop, Cash. And I don't know who it was, but she had black hair, black eyes, and a black heart. Anyway, that space is a nightmare. I had to shut her down. So, you know, thanks for calling in the tip I guess."

"I hear you saying I don't have to buy the first round after all."

"Did not say that." Ben hangs up and I laugh as I put the truck in gear to head home. If I'm not at the corner by the time the school bus arrives, there's no telling what Ruby might do.

If she's feeling sane, she might just wander home or make her way to the playground across the street from our house. But one time I was a little late and she had left her backpack on the curb to climb a wall and see if she could get up on the elevated train trestle. That one nearly gave me a stroke. I tried asking my mom for advice about that and she pointed out that my brother and I used to do the same stuff and basically implied I need to grow a tougher hide.

I lean against the street lamp post with my hands in my pockets, thinking about my leftover ache about having to come home with my tail between my legs once I dropped out of college. There was no way Heather and I could manage to stay in school *and* see to her health *and* prepare financially for a child.

Overnight, I went from someone who might act on the stage for his career, to falling right into the role my family always assumed I'd play in the workforce. I'm thankful my father made room for me in the electrician's apprenticeship program and got me situated with the union. I'm thankful for the paycheck that lets me and Ruby live comfortably in our own house while I only work whatever hours her public school is actually in session.

Which is not that much, let me tell you. Nobody ever explained that part to me—how short the school day is and how many days off they have for this and that and the other thing. I thought I'd be saving all kinds of money once Ruby was out of daycare, but it's probably a wash considering how much I reduced my hours.

The bus rumbles up and I wave as my daughter bounces out. She hollers goodbye to her friends as they all scatter and only once we're totally alone does she grab for my hand. Her teacher tells me this is all normal—calling me by my first name, not wanting to hold my hand in public. It still stings in comparison to her cuddling against my chest when she's injured.

She looks up at me and smiles. "How was your day, Cash?"

I squeeze her hand right back and notice she no longer has a bandage on. "Your finger feeling better?" She nods. "Good, good, and good."

I fish my keys out of my pocket and hold them out for her. "You want to be the one to unlock?"

"Yep!" I watch as her little tongue darts out as she sorts through all the keys and I smile along with her when she finds the right one to open the door. There's nothing quite like the feeling of watching my kid solve a problem, even a small one like learning how to unlock a door. It blows my mind that she's transforming from a totally dependent baby to...well, a kid who calls me Cash and knows how to jiggle the key and turn the deadbolt.

We both head to our rooms to change out of our uniforms and as I sit beside her to supervise her homework, my mind drifts to Ben shutting Piper down, and all the things I might do now that I'll have my peaceful morning hour back.

I already had to tell my PSA client I need an extension, but thankfully they said I could take until Monday. They happened to be swamped with requests at the moment and let me know I could snag a few other commercial spots if I wanted. Drink ads and self-help courses, mostly. After I talk Ruby through her spelling list I decide I'm going to accept the course gig. Hours and hours of voiceover income. I can choose any character I want to be for the narration...stern or encouraging. Energetic or monotone. My mind plays around with the options as my daughter and I make dinner, as I comb the snarls out of her hair, as she yells at me for being bad at braids.

I need this one thing, this escape hour in the morning to indulge these ridiculous fantasies. Because then I can come back to my real life, my important work of raising this kid, and I can give it my best effort.

So no. I don't feel bad at all that I sent Ben over there and he shut Piper down with all her loud music and asphalt-damaging bad habits.

Except, once I get Ruby tucked in for the night, I do imagine Piper's face when Ben delivered the news. But I can't handle the guilt that image brings, so I force myself to think about other things.

It doesn't go well.

10

PIPER

I SIGH FOR THE THOUSANDTH TIME, LOOKING AT THE spreadsheet Sam and Nicole helped me type up after I met with some contractors. I bought them cold-pressed juice and met them in the park mid-way between both their offices because neither of my corner-office pals could agree whose space was better for our brainstorm.

I am so proud of both of them for their boss-bitch status, and grateful for their expert input on my fledgling business. It's just that there are just so many zeroes on the estimate. I did not know I'd have to plan a major remodel in order to open. I lean against a tree in the park, trying to ignore the zeroes and waiting for my afternoon moms to arrive.

I had to shift some things around a bit since I can't accommodate my five AM class at all anymore. I lost all the clients with babies who nap in the afternoon, but the ones who have to rush off and meet a school bus were happy enough to work out in the park temporarily. Or so they said.

The thing is, I'm pretty much toast if I can't build up a bigger client list. And I can't build up a bigger client list without a space to bring them for workouts. Sure, the park is great for sunny afternoons. But it's autumn in Pittsburgh. It won't be long before we're all neck deep in wet leaves and random hail storms.

I smile as Sarah arrives, with her toddler in tow. I told her to go ahead and bring him, since we're right by the playground anyway. "There's a half day at school today," she says, checking her watch. "I've got an alarm set to dash off a few minutes early and meet the bus."

"No worries. I'm glad you got here!" I mean it, and feeling overwhelmed, I step in for a hug. Sarah is really freaking good at hugs, but I force myself to step back before things get awkward. I can never get enough hugging... another side effect to losing my mom so young.

A few more moms wander across the grass and I clap my hands to get organized. "Did everyone bring a towel?" They all nod and I get us set up with some stretches, using the towel to really lean into the upper body openers. "Feel that in your shoulders? I know all of you probably carry a lot of stress right there."

A chorus of appreciative groans surrounds me as I lead them all through what I call a mermaid stretch, with our legs bent out in front of us like a fish tail and our arms stretching the towel overhead. "Now, mermaids, dip forward and really feel that opening along your ribs. Yeah, that's the good stuff."

I notice Sarah's son is interested in what we're doing, so I give him my towel and he joins right in on the stretch. I smile, circling the group. I know I'm good at this. I know my clients really benefit from this work. I have to find a way to figure everything out. I just have to.

I cannot let Esther down, and equally important, I have to do it because of my mom.

If my own mother had had something like this, a group

encouraging her to work on herself, a group encouraging her to care for her body...things could have been different.

The little boy runs over to the playground and I get an idea. "All right, gals, on your feet." I start to run after Sarah's son. "Who remembers how to use the monkey bars?"

We're all a little too tall to really do any sort of pull-ups on the playground equipment, but I show everyone how to lean back on their heels to let the ground hold some (but not all) of their weight and use the bars for resistance. We climb the ladders up and down, lunge our way across the swinging bridge, and even use the swings to support some planks.

By the time Sarah and her kiddo duck out, nobody even notices that we're just a bunch of adults on the playground. It's good to hear everyone laughing, to see them all having so much fun while doing so much good work for their bodies.

"That's probably about enough for today." I smile and sink to the springy surface of the play equipment area. "That wasn't even on my original lesson plan, but I just felt like being a kid again."

Ayana laughs. "Don't tell *my* kids I almost did a pull-up. I don't want to have to do this again with people watching." She looks over her shoulder, as if she just remembered we are in a city park.

"Hate to tell you, Yana, but plenty of people probably saw you working that bod today." I bend forward to stretch my lower back and the class follows suit. "How's everyone doing with their goals?"

I share with the class that I did indeed visit the small business workshop at the library. "My next goal is finding an electrician for Pipe Fitters so we can get back indoors!"

Naomi and Ayana look at one another, seeming puzzled. "Why not just ask Cash?"

"Cash?"

"Ruby's dad," they say, like this is common knowledge. "Oh, there she is."

As if someone summoned her, a little girl wanders toward us through the grass, looking confused. Ayana waves. "Hey, Ruby. Remember me? I'm Emerald's mom."

"Oh." The girl's face relaxes a bit. "Hi. My dad's not home."

The class starts packing up their stuff to leave, noticing the time and panicking a bit about gathering children from early buses. Naomi and Ayana turn to Ruby. She looks familiar, and I remember that she was trying to join in with our class the first afternoon I led a session here in the park.

Naomi purses her lips. "Do you have your dad's number? I don't think I have him in my phone."

Ruby shakes her head. "I think maybe he forgot we had a half day at school."

Naomi and Ayana seem concerned. "Should we walk over with you and check the door again? Maybe he was in the shower!"

Ruby bites her lip and I realize she must live right nearby.

"I'll hang with Ruby until we can find her dad. I have some stuff to do for Pipe Fitters anyway." I see Naomi visibly relax, and I know the two of them need to get off to take care of their families. "It's okay. Ruby and I will get to know each other as neighbors."

My students wave and make their way to their cars as Ruby tugs on her school uniform. "Are we neighbors? I saw you in the park before."

"Well, I don't live here, but my business is back there." I point to the alley. "Want to see?"

"Oh," Ruby says falling in step with me. "Are you the loud lady from the alley?"

I feel a flush creep up my cheeks and I wince. "I guess I wasn't being super considerate with my music when I first opened."

Ruby shrugs. "My dad gets cranky in the morning. That's his word. Grandma calls him pissy."

I laugh, startled to hear a curse word emerge from such a little kid. "Well," I tell her. "I get a little grumpy when I get woken up, too. I promise to be quieter. How's that?"

"What do you do in there anyway?" Ruby puts her hands on her hips and looks at the warehouse space threatening to bankrupt me.

"At the moment, not much. But if you want, we can hit a tire with a sledge hammer."

Her eyes go wide and she claps her hands. "That sounds amazing!"

11

CASH

Something seems off. I've been waiting at Ruby's bus stop for over 15 minutes and there are no other parents around. I don't have a text or anything from the school about the bus being delayed. It seems unlikely that it was early, but I figure I better head toward the playground to check for Ruby just in case.

When I walk down there, I see a bunch of kids running around throwing mulch at each other, but Ruby isn't one of them. A few of the other parents wave at me and I freeze. They should be at the bus stop, but there they all are at the playground. With their kids.

And Ruby is nowhere to be seen.

I take a deep breath, hoping maybe Ruby set my phone to another time zone or something.

I'll just walk back to the bus stop and check one more time. *This is fine. This is fine.*

I decide to take the alley back to the bus stop, maybe peek in my back yard to check for Ruby. And that's when I see it.

My child swinging a sledge hammer.

In an alley. Where cars drive. My blood turns to ice as I start running toward her.

She hoists the weapon over her head and I sprint toward her, screaming for her to stop.

Ruby looks at me, startled, and drops the hammer. It bounces off the rubber tire in front of her and mercifully hits the street and not my little girl.

"What in the hell are you doing?" I don't even realize who I'm yelling at until my eyes focus. It's Piper. Of course it's Piper. "You handed a dangerous weapon to my child? What is wrong with you?"

She seems perplexed, looking back and forth between Ruby and me. "Your child?"

I crouch and put my hands on Ruby's shoulders, checking her all over for bruises. "Are you okay? What on earth are you doing back here? I've been waiting at your bus stop!"

Ruby beams, totally unbothered by any of the nightmare visions currently choking me. "Piper and me are hitting tires!" Ruby kicks the tire for emphasis and then moves to climb on top of it. "Piper flipped this out here herself from inside her gym. Do you know she can do a pull-up?"

I'm at a loss for words. I have no idea how my kid managed to get back here without me seeing her get off the bus. I have no idea why a reasonable adult would hand a small child a sledge hammer. I should have called the cops the other night instead of Ben. "I'm going to call the police," is what I manage to mutter, reaching in my work pants in search of my phone. "You should be incarcerated. I should never have stopped at the building inspector."

Piper gasps and Ruby starts making a siren sound. "Police! Stop! He's getting away." She starts running in circles around the alley, kicking the tire each time she passes me. Flustered, I drop my phone and stoop to gather it before Ruby steps on it.

"*You* called the building inspector?" Piper's voice sounds about like mine—angry and low, like barely contained rage. "Why would you do that?"

"Let's not play games here. You're operating a business out of a dangerous facility. You're violating the noise ordinance. You're damaging the street surface my tax dollars paid for. And for some unknown reason you've decided to hand a fucking—flipping—sledge hammer to a seven-year-old child. You have no business being—"

"Unknown reason?" Her eyes flash as she interrupts me. She picks up the handle of the sledge hammer and I'm not entirely sure she doesn't intend to swing it at me. I step in front of Ruby, protectively. Piper shrieks. "The *reason* is that your kid was wandering around the park unattended. Please do call the police so I can tell them you neglected your daughter when she had a half day of school!"

"Police! Open up!" Ruby pounds her fist against our garage door.

Did Piper say half day?

"Fuck!" I drag a hand through my hair and take a step back from Piper, who is still holding the sledge hammer. As soon as I yell this obscenity, Ruby halts in her tracks and stares at me and my elderly neighbor sticks her head out the window and shouts into the alley.

"Cashel Brennan, there's no cause to yell profanity! This is a family neighborhood." She frowns, and then sees Ruby and smiles. "Hello, Ruby, dear. Did I see you over at the playground alone again?"

Ruby cups her hands over her mouth. "I wasn't alone, Mrs. Kochinsky! I was playing with my friend Piper." Ruby hooks a thumb over her shoulder at the woman in question, who has now hoisted the sledge hammer over her shoulder and looks a little like Xena.

Mrs. Kochinsky surveys the scene in the alley and waves her hand. "Just keep it down out there, all of you." She slams the window shut and her curtains flash white like the truce flag I might need as I start piecing all this together.

"Half day?" I mutter it again and look over at Ruby, who is now jumping on the tire like it's a trampoline.

Ruby nods. "Half day. 'Member how I didn't need shoes for gym today?"

My stomach sinks as I do remember her saying that. I finally get my phone working and pull up the calendar and...sure enough, today is labeled bright orange. HALF DAY. It's right there and...I missed it.

I sink down onto the tire, not caring that I'm sitting in the middle of an alley. Where cars drive. But pretty rarely. "Ruby, babe. I'm so, so sorry. Are you okay? Were you scared?"

Piper remains standing in the alley with the sledge hammer, Xena-style. I swallow in concern as Ruby says, "I was scared at first because the door was locked. But then I went to the playground and Piper was there playing with some ladies." Ruby looks up at Piper. "How come you weren't dancing this time? I never saw grownups use the zip line..."

Piper smiles and finally lowers the sledge hammer to the ground, resting it against the tire. "I was teaching a class. I think some of my students have kids at your school. They had to leave early to meet the bus."

She emphasizes the word early and her eyes dart to me. It becomes clear that I now need to thank her. Profusely. And...probably apologize. "Shit," I say instead.

Ruby gasps and starts yelling, "You said a red word! That's a red word again!"

Piper's not done, though. She smiles a giant, fake grin and tells Ruby, "We were playing in the park because I'm not allowed to have students in my gym." She points lovingly to the crusty space that should be condemned. "I had to think of some new ideas to help the moms move their bodies for their healthy hearts."

"Hm," Ruby taps her chin like she's trying to help Piper think of ideas. "You could have them play blob tag. Do you ever play that?"

I stand up and put a hand on her shoulder. "Hey, Rubes, I think we ought to go inside and change and make a plan for dinner."

Ruby looks up at me, eyes wide. "We should take Piper to dinner. Play dates usually include a meal."

"Oh, sweetie, this wasn't a play date." I try to steer her toward the house where I can take my time and muster the will to eat crow and apologize to Piper. "You were barely safe," I mutter.

"Hey!" I turn to see Piper standing with her arms crossed and brow furrowed. "Don't you dare talk that way about safety. I'm fully certified in the types of fitness I coach, for youth and adults. I would never, ever knowingly put a client in danger. Paid or otherwise."

"I didn't mean to—"

Piper literally gives me the hand, cutting me off again. "Ruby joined my class and was my student for the afternoon. She was absolutely safe at all times. If you like I can submit a copy of my PA state clearances to work with children. But don't you dare imply anyone is unsafe on my watch."

Her nostrils flare in and out and what I should do is nod

my head and tell her she's right. But what I do instead is lean into my frustration from a long week without enough work hours, at my embarrassment for losing track of the time and missing my kid's school bus. What I say is, "Pretty sure the city of Pittsburgh officially declared your business unsafe." I point at the orange notice taped to her business door and turn on my boot heel, hoping to God Ruby follows me inside the house.

12

PIPER

I EMAIL MY STUDENTS FROM INSIDE MY FALLING-DOWN GYM TO cancel my evening class because I just can't get it together to teach fitness right now. I'm feeling a combination of murderous and sad and I'm not sure what to do about it. But then, bless them, my afternoon students start texting me to ask if I ever found Ruby's dad.

All it takes is a few mad face emojis for them to ask where I'll be so they can come give me a hug.

My students! Want to give me a hug. These women really do give me life. I decide, as per usual, to head to Bridges and Bitters to see if Esther can cheer me up. Or liquor me up. Whichever is easier.

I arrive as Esther is pouring out glasses of her Fall Fireball Cocktail, but I wrinkle my nose at the idea of cinnamon whiskey today. Esther taps her fingers on the edge of the bar, considering me in my workout gear, sweating on my stool as I vibrate with emotion.

"I know what I'm making you," she says, just as a trio of Pipe Fitters students bursts in the door of the bar. "She's over here, gals," Esther shouts, pointing to me as my students clamor toward me.

Ayana squeezes my hand. "What happened, Pipes? Toia said you're canceling class..."

Fatima, another regular student of mine, pulls her stool close to me on the other side and leans on the bar. She rests her olive chin on her fists, rapt.

"Oh." I sigh. "Well. I've had some snafus."

Esther pops up with a silver cocktail shaker. "How about Pear-ly Contained Rage?" She slides some sliced fruit into the shaker. "Bourbon—good-ass bourbon for you, pet— muddled pear, lemon juice, rosemary syrup." She pours the dark, fragrant liquid into a glass and pops a sprig of rosemary in for a garnish. "Drink up."

Fatima slaps her palm on the bar. "That smells amazing. I'll have one, too." She looks at me as I sip the drink. The whiskey tingles my tongue but I feel immediately warm and more relaxed after my first sip. Maybe it's just that I'm surrounded by people who care about me now.

"Okay, so the thing is, I found out that a person called the building inspector on me. On purpose. Knowing I'd get shut down."

"Back up." Ayana arches a brow at me and her eyes flash in anger. "Someone ratted you out to the city? About our gym?"

"I love that you call it ours." I pat Ayana's arm. "I feel that way, too. But yes. Someone...tattled. I knew the electricity was bad! I was starting to gather info to fix all that stuff but now..."

I drift off and take another sip of my drink. The fruit and herbs taste so sweet and delicate blended with the spice of the whiskey. "Esther, I really think this is a perfect drink. Absolutely marvelous."

Esther grins and pulls a notebook from her back pocket. She always writes her drink ideas down by hand before she commits them to her seasonal menus. Sam has tried and tried to get Esther to use a data management system so she can track stuff about the drinks. But Esther isn't interested. I sort of like watching the two of them grapple about the necessity of big data in an industry like mixology.

Naomi finishes her own glass of Pear-ly Contained Rage and purses her lips. She looks at Esther and then back at Ayana and Fatima. "I have a theory about who ratted you out."

Feeling a little tipsy now after the strong drink, I hiccup and point a finger in the air. "I think my friend Sam would say you have a hypothesis. Not a theory."

Naomi pokes me in the leg. "Okay, but here's what I'm thinking. Cash Brennan woke up on the wrong side of the bed one morning when we were rocking out over in Pipe Fitters and he called one of his buddies to come 'check out' your business." She turns to Fatima. "Remember when Cash came out and kicked that trash can? You tell me I'm wrong."

I gulp and nod slowly. "He told me as much this afternoon. That was just the final straw for my day. And I took care of Ruby. Did you know he has a daughter? And that Ruby is the daughter? He's a giant man-dad." I hiccup again as my students start up a chorus of "mm hmm" and "oh, we know all about it."

Fatima slams her empty glass on the bar. "I'm giving him last pick for room parent jobs. His kid's in class with my son. He's about to stock tissues and hand sanitizer for months."

"No," Ayana taps a finger on the bar. "Make him change out the play dough. That shit is full of boogers and bacteria."

I smile weakly at my students. "You guys, I don't want to get revenge like that. I just need to figure out a way to not go bank—" I stop, realizing I'm about to reveal the depths of my business problems to my students. That's not a fair burden to place on them. "I just don't want to go low, you know?"

Esther slides back from delivering a tray of drinks to some other customers. "You plotting revenge?" She directs this question not at me but the women who suddenly have a lot to say about a lot of tiny, petty things they want to do to get back at the ginger grump who ratted me out.

As Ayana and Fatima and Namoi list out their plans, I realize that elementary school moms can be really flipping fierce if they set their minds to it. I blink as I listen to their plans to make sure Cash is working the PTA bake sale early morning shift when the school is used for a polling place on Election Day.

Esther cackles. "You bitches are brutal." She slides them each another round of Pear-ly Contained Rage and winks. "On the house for broads who back my buddy."

I straighten my ponytail to cover up the fact that I'm near tears. "You guys," I choke out. "I appreciate all of this, but I just want to run my business, you know? I'm here for YOU. I just want to help people lead healthier lives...longer lives."

My clients bump shoulders with me at the bar. "We know that. But we want *you* to know that your service really matters to us." Naomi pats my hand.

Ayana nods. "You saw what those other jerks were like when we tried to go to the gym. Sure, they had childcare there, but I have no idea how to work any of that fancy equipment. And I don't want to tell some young dude that I pee when I jump rope." She lowers her voice. "Thank you for that PT recommendation, by the way, Piper. Things are getting better."

I smile. "I knew Betty could help. I'm going to do a training with her to learn some things I can incorporate in my classes."

"You see?" Fatima waves a hand around me. "You're what the moms of Pittsburgh need, Piper. We need you, and if Cash Brennan is gonna mess up my chance to get a better bladder, then I'm sure as hell going to make his life hard however I can." She nods, as if this is the final word.

I sigh and enjoy my drink until Naomi's wife arrives to drive us all home.

13

CASH

I FEEL SUCH A SENSE OF RELIEF WHEN MY MOM ARRIVES TO pick Ruby up for their shopping and sleepover adventure. And then I feel like shit for feeling relieved. But it's down to me if she stays safe or gets hurt. I'm the only one responsible, and I hadn't realized how much I've been holding my breath every second, worried Ruby will hurt herself or wander off.

I guess what I really need to worry about is whether I'm going to forget her again. Fuck. Frick. Whatever. The first thing I need to do is sit down and update my calendar on my phone and set all sorts of alarms for all these damn days off school.

But the first thing I actually do is rush out to the garage to finish this project for my client. I jump around for a bit, chewing on green apple slices and clucking my tongue to warm up. And then I slip on the headphones, fire up the mic, and bang the project out.

Barely an hour has passed. That's all I needed, was an hour. Why can't I find one frickin hour without shipping my kid off to my mom?

On paper, it makes sense. I basically work part-time but I earn enough to keep us comfortable here. Ruby's a good kid...she's just a kid. But eventually I should be able to hide in the garage for an hour while she does something on her own, right?

I sigh, wishing for the millionth time that I had someone I could share all this with, and then I chastise myself for wishing again. Wishes don't get me anywhere. But work does, and I've got time to work right now, so I better not waste it.

I head inside to my computer where I can edit the files in a bit more comfort and I ship the whole thing off with plenty of time to spare before I'm apparently buying Ben a bunch of drinks.

I see a flash of something in the alley and I glance out the window above my monitor to see Piper dragging shit around. It looks like she's emptying out her space and I feel a twinge of shame, remembering how I spoke to her yesterday. Fuck, she was the responsible adult looking out for my kid and I attacked her...after I sent the building inspector after her and got her business shut down.

I rub a hand through my beard, wondering if her clean out is permanent or if she's just moving shit to make room for a contractor. I really do owe her an apology but I can't bring myself to walk out there and offer it to her because I'm attracted to her and I don't want to be. I have no business lusting after when it's all I can do to raise my kid.

Plus I'm dealing with all this guilt even though she messed with *my* business first. Not my business...my hobby. Or, to use my parents' lingo, my "little hobby." It was a big deal for me to buck the family trade tradition and try an "artsy fartsy college." I was back, with Ruby in tow, before I really had a chance to try and fail.

I need to stop ogling Piper and get to the bar. I hope Ben isn't there with a group or planning to try and set me up with someone. I have no capacity for that right now. I can't even remember what women smell like.

That's not entirely true. I caught a whiff of Piper the other day when she swung that sledge hammer at me. She smelled like sweat and salt and totally off limits. Damn, though, she looks good in her workout gear.

It doesn't even seem like she's aware of it. She just moves through the world so confidently, like she owns the space. Like she's got no care in the world.

Except I know that's not true. Piper does care about her business and anyone can see that's in trouble...and it's not entirely my fault. Not really. It's actually not safe to have people inside that crumbling box if the electrical is messed up.

Rather than listen to the tiny voice in my head reminding me I could help her with that exact problem, I decide to shower and get ready. My amends to Piper can wait another day while I find the right words to say.

14

PIPER

I'M SPENDING MY WEEKEND EVENING AT PIPE FITTERS, LIKE any reasonable business owner. I have been burning the candle at both ends to see if I can finally map out a plan of action. Between the library chats, the women in class, and Esther, I feel like I can make a pretty solid to-do list to get my doors back open.

If I'm working on a to-do list, I'm not fighting off fears of failure. I need this place to succeed, not just because I'm financially invested but because I need it to exist for the women I serve.

My mom spent her entire life taking care of everyone but herself. She was the ultimate cheerleader for me and my brother, hauling us to all our activities and even showing up to cheer for us when we played sports in college. Meanwhile, she wasn't taking care of herself at all. Sitting on all those sidelines for all that time...of course she didn't have any extra time for exercise. I brush away a stray tear as I drive to my gym, thinking about the hospital reports after she died.

We had no idea she was in such poor cardiovascular

health. Mostly because she never bothered with her annual physicals and bloodwork. I just know that I can create a space for moms to really get a handle on their health.

That's been my driving goal ever since: to help women be healthy.

Not everyone can invest the time and energy to become a ninja warrior. My gym isn't about that. I want to teach people ways to incorporate movement into their lives, to build lasting healthy habits that work for them.

Every kid should be able to grow up with their parent there to celebrate their achievements.

"I will not fail," I mutter to my mother's energy in the atmosphere.

I unlock the door to Pipe Fitters and turn the lights on, but that doesn't last long because there's a loud pop and one of them goes out in a shower of sparks. I sigh. This is not a deterrent! Did the landlord bamboozle me into an inferior rental? Yes. But he isn't the first man to dick me over and I can't let that stand in my way.

Before long, I'm set up with my portable speaker rocking out to my concentration playlist. I scan my notes for low-hanging fruit I can take care of quickly to get this space up and running again...but it all seems like unripe, gnarled fruit way up at the top of the tree...

The light flickers again and I note that I need to book an electrician first-thing on Monday. I think one of the women from FOOF can hook me up with a general contractor, so that goes on my must-do list as well.

After a bit, I stop noticing the cold floor and the slight ache in my tailbone as I work, abandoning the to-do list for some lesson plans and backup plans if the weather is too bad for a park workout.

I'm bent over with my ass in the air, practicing a move, when my door hinges creak.

"Fuuuck." I hear a familiar voice and whip my head to the open door to see the grumpy Sasquatch, bane of my existence.

I don't bother standing up, but continue making notes on my workout lesson plans as I say, "Haven't you done enough damage over here?"

Cash leans against the wall after closing the door behind him. He crosses his beefy arms over his chest and I don't miss how his forearms strain delectably beneath that fur of red hair. "I didn't think you'd be over here this late."

I roll my eyes at him, seriously. Cash is not invited to criticize. "I'll knock on your door when I need your advice about my work schedule," I manage to say, making note of my comeback to share with the girls later.

Cash's gaze stays trained on me as I squat down and save all my files before logging out of my computer. There's something different about him right now..."Are you drunk?" I walk over toward him and sniff, catching a whiff of tangy hops.

He rocks his hand side to side in a "so-so" motion, but doesn't stop staring at me. I straighten out my hair and smooth my hands down my pants, brushing a little dust off my legs as Cash scrutinizes every motion. Two can play at this game. I stand up and drink him in with my eyes, from his boots and well-worn jeans that cling to his thighs and butt, to the solid chest and freckled forearms. His body has clearly been carved by hard work, not just the gym. And if I had to guess, I'd say Cash Brennan has amazing, beefy thighs.

"Like what you see, Piper?"

I snort. "Okay, now that we've both finished staring at one another, you can go on home. I won't bother you with music in the morning, all right? You took care of that." I manage to ward off a shudder when I think about my location being closed, even if temporarily.

Cash lets his head fall back against the wall with a dull thunk. He closes his eyes and swallows and damn it! Even his throat is attractive. I remind myself that even jerks can be attractive. And make no mistake. Cash Brennan has been an asshole to me.

"I've been an asshole," he says, and I gasp, which startles him. We stare at one another again, wide-eyed. His face softens and I smell the beer on his breath. I get the sense he's not used to feeling buzzed. "I've been an asshole," he repeats. "I owe you...amends."

I scrunch my face up in confusion. "Amends? Is that like an apology?"

He grunts. The lights pop again and Cash slaps the wall. "Amends is where I get your electrical up to code for you and you stop making that face."

I puff out a laugh. "Why would I hire you to fix my electrical? You'd probably make it worse on purpose."

Cash shoves his hands in his pockets and shrugs. "You didn't have to take care of Ruby. But you did. So now I'll fix your wiring. And trust me, Piper. I'm the best." One of the lights flashes back on triumphantly, as if it wants Cash's hands all over it. I look at his hands, big and thick as they stick out of his pockets. I shake my head. *Stop it, Piper. We do not ogle the Sasquatch.*

"I'd never leave a child alone in the park."

Cash slumps to the floor and puts his elbows on his bent knees, banging his forehead off his fists. "I can't believe I fucked up like that. She must have been so scared." His face looks raw and vulnerable, and damn it, I can't let him drown in guilt. I plunk down on the ground next to him, putting a hand on his knee.

"Hey." I give him a squeeze. "She wasn't scared."

15

CASH

EVEN IN MY HALF-DRUNK HAZE, I CAN TELL THAT I'M attracted to this woman. It's hopeless. Despite her loud music and clown car and too-casual attitude about building safety. I try to tell my libido it's just been awhile, that anyone would be attracted to this woman with her firm everything and her tight pants.

But it's more than that.

I screwed her over, and she took care of my kid anyway, not to gloat or lord it over me. She just fucking cares about people.

It's all I can do not to reach out and pull Piper into my lap and kiss the hell out of her here on the floor in this catastrophe waiting to happen.

I hurry to my feet before I do anything dumb. "If you leave me a key, I can come in here Monday after work and assess your wiring." I gesture toward the door, assuming she'll walk out first and lock up and we'll both be on our way. But she just squats there on the ground looking up at me like I'm the weird one in this situation.

"Did you miss the part where you pretty much ruined

my life and acted like a big jerk-face? Why would I let you touch my wires?"

I suck air in through my teeth. This is not going as expected. To be fair to myself, the only women I really talk to are customers and my seven-year-old. They all view me as a bit of an authority figure. "You will let me repair your electrical because I'm going to do it for free...well, for the cost of parts, but I get those cheap. What's the issue here?"

Piper stands and puts her hands on her hips. I absolutely do not look twice at the effect this movement has on her breasts. No, I do not take note of how firm they look or... fuck it all, I can see her nipples even in this flickering light. "Cash Brennan, if that's your real name, the issue is that you are mean and you were rude and I...well, I just don't like you."

I lean forward and look her in the eye. She blows a tuft of stray hair away from her face. I watch as her pupils widen the closer I get. "Liar," I whisper.

She rolls her eyes and lets out a sigh. Her breath smells like fruity gum. "Okay, fine, but I'm trying very hard not to like you. You, as I said, were unkind to me. I do not make space in my life for unkind people."

I can't tell if she means it or if she's just repeating that until she believes whatever guru gave her that advice. Either way, she has a point. I need to actually apologize to her. I close my eyes and swallow, and when I open my eyes again, I see she's staring at my neck.

"You're right, Piper. I behaved badly and I acted rashly and you've been nothing but kind to my daughter and I apologize. Can I please make it up to you by repairing your wiring?"

She blinks at me and I wonder if I actually managed to say all that or just imagined myself apologizing. "How do I know you're really an electrician? What if you're just saying all this to get your Ben buddy back in here with more fines?"

"He gave you a fine?" Did he mention that part to me? I'm a little too buzzed for this conversation.

She rolls her eyes. "He took it back. Eventually."

I laugh and then fish in my jeans pocket for my wallet. "I've got my union card in here somewhere. I'm certified. Haven't you seen my truck?"

She snorts and it's adorable. I want to reach out and boop her nose, and then I remember I'm in the middle of amends here. Piper wrinkles that button nose. "How do I know you didn't just steal the truck to make it *look* like you're an electrician?" I arch a brow at her and cross my arms, leaning against the wall because it's cool, not because I need it to hold me up. "That was...okay, well...gah. Fine." She slaps a key in my hand. I note that her key ring is a rusty old pipe coupling. I hold it up and stare at it, squinting.

Piper shuffles around the space and when I look at her again, she's wearing a hoodie and has a bag slung over one shoulder. "Okay, well, I'm going to bed." She taps her toe and bites her lip. "You'll lock up?"

I nod and stare at her as she walks over to her Fiat. She waves as she drives slowly down the alley before turning onto Dallas Ave.

RUBY GIVES me a lecture on timeliness Monday morning, and I'm at the bus stop that afternoon nice and early. I give her a salute as she pops off the bus with a nod. "Hey, Cash." She starts walking toward the house and I ruffle her hair, giving up on asking her to ever call me Dad. I sort of like that she thinks of me as a friend.

"We've got some plans this afternoon, Rubes." I fumble in my pocket for the house keys and jiggle the expanded key ring, which now also contains Piper's stuff. "I'm helping Piper with some electrical work."

Ruby claps her hands. "Do I get to swing the sledge hammer again?" She throws her backpack on the ground and jumps up and down.

I shake my head. "You absolutely do not get to do that. You'll be hanging out in *our* garage, nice and safe."

She frowns and puts her hands on her hips. "Piper let me swing the sledge hammer. She has all kinds of stuff in there."

"I'm sure she does." I gesture for Ruby to pick up her bag and hang it on the hook. Our house is far from pristine, but we can both at least manage to keep our bags off the floor. "The thing is, she needs all new wiring in there."

"How do you know? Did you start already?"

"I can just tell. I'm going to need the big lights." Ruby's eyes widen and she nods. She loves when I have to pull out the battery-operated work lamps. Ruby likes to pretend she's a movie star or something. Sometimes I find her dancing to the damn Kid Bop videos with the work lights blaring in our living room.

I shoo her upstairs to change while I gather up the supplies I think I'll need to get going across the alley. She's up and down in under a minute, and I'm pretty sure she tossed her clothes on the ground, but we can deal with that later. "We're burning daylight here." I sigh as I realize I am regurgitating my father's catch phrases to my own kid. I open up the back door and Ruby trails behind me, happily carrying one of the lamps.

We set everything down in the alley and I unlock Pipe Fitters. I roll up the garage door for added daylight and turn to Ruby, my expression stern. "You will not come in here unless I tell you it's safe. You will stay on our side of the alley. Got it?"

She nods. "Got it."

Ruby mutters to herself as I set up the lights and a ladder. I locate the access panel and shake my head at the shitty workmanship I find inside. If the circuit breakers are a budget brand known for poor performance, what am I going to find inside those walls?

A better question would be when on earth I'm going to find the time to work on this for free. Ruby can't be expected to entertain herself for the amount of hours this will take. Well. She's okay for right now I guess. I brought this challenge on myself. I groan at the sight of a frayed wire and try to stifle my rage that Piper could have been harmed, and also that Piper has put me in this position.

I shut off the power to her space and get to work.

16

PIPER

I CAN'T HELP MYSELF. I HAVE TO STOP BY THE ALLEY AND SEE what Cash is doing...or not doing to my gym. I leave my car at the park after my afternoon class and walk back to Pipe Fitters. I do like the sound of that, even if my gym is closed and sort of in peril at the moment.

I grin when I see Ruby dancing around in her garage. I wave and her face lights up. "Piper! Want to come dance with me?" As I get closer, I can see that she's set up all kinds of equipment and is having quite the studio experience in her garage.

"This is...wow. This is pretty high tech."

Ruby twirls and points at a curtain hanging in one corner of the garage. "This is all my dad's stuff. I'm not supposed to touch it."

I frown. "But you definitely touched it, right?"

She shrugs and points at my gym. "He's in there doing electric things and I'm not supposed to go over there."

I hear the sound of a drill, followed by a clattering, slinking noise. I wince. "It's probably safer if we stay over here. But you're sure you didn't damage anything your dad was working on?" I walk over to the curtain and peek inside the space where the edges don't quite meet. It's some sort of dressing room with privacy curtains, complete with a microphone I think I saw him throw a few days ago. "What is all this?"

Cash has a whole host of sound equipment set up, and I'm fairly certain this isn't the stuff he'd use day to day as an electrician.

Ruby turns the volume down on the music and opens the shower curtain. "This is Cash's sound booth. For his voice stuff."

"Voice stuff?" I look over her head at the music stand where he's got a notebook and a battered pair of headphones. "Does he sing?" Lord help me if that gigantic man can also sing. I remind myself that he's mean.

"He sings to me," she says, proudly. "This is for his talking jobs."

Before Ruby can elaborate, I hear a clang from my gym and the two of us whip our heads around to see Cash wrestling with a spool of wire. He seems to be muttering curses under his breath. I walk toward him, gingerly. "That bad?"

He looks up and notices me and I think perhaps he almost smiles briefly before his face sags back into his permanent scowl. "It's a whole patchwork nightmare in there."

I glance up and see he's cut only a small hole in the ceiling. I also see the tool belt slung around his hips and the curve of his ass in his dark blue Dickies. I literally have to fan myself, but I make it look like I'm waving dust away. "I thought you'd have to rip all the walls down."

"Nah. I told you. I'm good at this." Cash tosses a length of wire to the side triumphantly. It all looks dusty and older than me. "Gonna take some time, though." He scowls up at the sky, seeing that the light is fading. "I gotta get Ruby her dinner and put her to bed."

"Piper should put me to bed," Ruby announces, appearing at Piper's side. Cash points at her, but she frowns. "I'm not in the gym. I'm outside the gym. And I want Piper to read to me tonight."

I grin. "That does sound nice. But it sounds like your dad needs a rest. I think that's why—"

"I never said I was tired." Cash seems to take offense at the suggestion that he might need a break after working all day and then apparently pulling out all of the old wiring in my business.

I shrug my shoulders. "Sorry. I just...I guess..."

Ruby squeezes my hand. "We can make dinner together. And you can keep growling at the wires!"

"Oh, honey, I'm not sure if I should go—okay." I follow along as my arm is tugged toward the house. Ruby bursts in the back door of a tidy rowhouse, pulling me into a yellow kitchen with mismatched appliances. I'm not sure what to make of the warm feelings creeping over me when I observe there are no dirty dishes in the sink, no stains on the counters. There's a spice rack above the gas range, and it all looks well-used but clean.

I feel like an intruder and it's strange to think of this private side of Cash, that this tidy room is where he makes his lunch each day and talks to his daughter about school.

"What should we cook?" Ruby opens the refrigerator and looks to me like I have any kind of idea what their plans were for meals.

"Um, what do you usually eat on a Monday?" I glance inside to see bags of carrots and apples, a few condiments, and several packages of meat, among other staples. Cash is better at stocking his fridge than my friend Samantha. This makes me laugh. I love all the ways people are complex.

Ruby taps her lip. "We should do spaghetti. Tomorrow is tacos. Except we don't like shells. Cash and I do bowls with nacho chips and just *call* it tacos."

"Seems reasonable." I slide a package of ground meat from the fridge and hold it up for Ruby to inspect. "Should we do meat in the sauce?" She nods her head and I set it on the counter. "Why do you call your dad Cash?"

She shrugs. "He has a neat name."

"Hm." I roll up my sleeves. "I'm trying to imagine what my dad would say if I called him by his first name."

"Is he mean?" Ruby's eyes go wide and she halts, her arms laden with pantry goods.

"Oh, no, he's not mean. But he'd definitely think it was disrespectful. I think that's it. But I guess kids today call a lot of grownups by their first names, huh?"

As Ruby pulls out a box of pasta and a jar of sauce, I snag a pan from the hooks on the wall. We wash our hands and get to work, and it just feels so...normal. Ruby informs me, "My teacher at school says we should call her Suzy. And the bus driver is Ashley."

I nod. "Those are important adults. With cool names!"

She smiles, like that's the end of that, and starts telling me about a raccoon who runs around the gutters.

I realize I wasn't too much older than Ruby when my own mother died, and that my memories of doing this sort of thing with her all stop right around middle school.

My heart catches in my throat, and time seems to stand still before I can compose myself. Ruby looks up at me, confused, so I smile at her and shake out my arms. "Got lost in my thoughts there for a minute."

We decide to add some seasoning to the sauce and I

convince Ruby that we can puree some of the spinach I find in the fridge and stir it in and she won't even notice the taste. She eyes me skeptically but after a few minutes of simmering with the meat and herbs, the sauce seems blended enough that I give her a taste. Her eyes fly wide and she grins. "I'm eating spinach!"

"How about that?"

BY THE TIME we get out the plates and strain the noodles, Cash is hauling himself through the back door. There's really no other word to describe how he moves, giant bear of a man that he is. He looks at Ruby and I standing by the stove and seems like he is also overcome with emotion for a second, before the mask of grumpiness settles back onto his features. "I'm going to stop for the day," he says, gesturing outside. "I need to pick up some supplies."

"Oh. Well, if you make me a list I can grab it. You shouldn't have to pay money to fix—"

He holds up a hand. "I get stuff at a bulk discount through the business. I told you I'd handle it." He washes his hands and strides into the dining room. I realize that I'm not angry with him right now. Quite the contrary, in fact. I'm a little blown away by his thoughtfulness, inside the grumpy exterior. I hear the scrape of a chair being pulled out and take that as my cue to follow Ruby out of the kitchen, a bowl of steaming noodles hiding the stunned expression on my face.

17

CASH

THERE'S A WOMAN IN MY HOUSE AND I CAN BARELY BREATHE because of it.

Not just any woman. *That* woman. The one who's been vexing me. It's not bad enough that I owe her an electrical repair. Oh, no. Now my kid has invited her inside and she's standing next to my daughter making sauce like a mother might do.

It's too much. Something has to be done here.

This life I built for me and Ruby only works if we stick to the path. Noses down, working hard. There's no room here for women. There just isn't.

I'm about to kick her out when Ruby splashes a ladle of sauce onto my plate. "Guess what's in there? You won't guess. It's spinach."

She sticks her finger into her own plop of sauce and licks it off with gusto. I arch a brow at her. "You're eating spinach?"

She nods. "It's good when you stir it in. See? It's not even green." Ruby points at the sauce. It just looks like regular sauce to me, although I see that she and Piper used tomorrow's taco meat to make it. That means I'll have to use Wednesday's chicken for the tacos and lord knows what I'll do for dinner come Wednesday. I sigh again. I am not cut out for all this last-minute change. It's too much.

I'm hanging on by a wire. I think I've known that for a long time.

Piper twirls her pasta on her fork and smiles as she slides it into her mouth. Is she being suggestive on purpose, putting her lips around the fork that way? Or do her lips just look like that...plump and kissable. *Fuck me.*

It makes sense that I'm attracted to her. I decide it's safer that way, too. If all this buzz in my veins is just my libido, then everything can go back to how it was. There are lots of attractive women.

I clear my throat. "I have to know." I lean forward toward our house guest. "What made a person like you drive past *that* space out there and then sign a lease?"

"Someone like me? What's that mean?"

I shake my head and fork myself a mouthful of pasta. Shit, it's good. What did she do to this sauce? "I mean someone sort of fancy."

Piper laughs. "I'm not fancy! I wear leggings to work."

I grunt out a half laugh. "But how much did you pay for the leggings?"

Piper blows out a long breath through her nose. "To go back to your original question, I needed to get out of my job situation very quickly. Opening a business had been part of my plan, but I had to jump the gun." She shrugs. "It's not the space I would have envisioned, but I think it fits."

I sigh and eat another bite of food. It really is the best spaghetti I've had in a long time. "Alessio shouldn't be renting the space out in that condition." I growl at the idea of him taking advantage of tenants like Piper, people with ideas.

But since when am I defending her?

I look over at Ruby, who has eaten an entire bowl of food and has sauce staining her face. "You like this?"

She nods. "Piper let me add the oregano. And we added garlic. Lots of garlic."

"Garlic fixes everything," Piper says, definitively.

I want to ask her what she meant by getting out of a job situation quickly. I want to ask her about her plans and how she got my daughter to eat spinach. But those are the sorts of questions that lead to friendship, that come with expectations. And I can't meet anyone's expectations except my daughter's. I'm just attracted to her. Because she's hot.

I open my mouth to ask Piper to leave and give us some privacy for bedtime, but Ruby springs up from the table and clangs over to her backpack. "I need help with my math facts." She's back and in her seat in such a frenzy that I forget I'm supposed to be kicking out the beautiful woman I called the city on. "Piper, are you good at math facts?"

Ruby pulls a gnawed up pencil from her folder and starts tapping it loudly against the table.

Piper grins. "I am actually pretty great at math facts. I use a lot of math when I'm designing exercise plans. Let me see." I peer over the pasta dish and see that Ruby's working on subtraction this week. She struggles with subtraction. Piper starts to quiz her on the problems and I have nothing to do but growl at my pasta as the two of them fly through homework that would take me an hour of arguing with my daughter.

I notice Piper make an uncomfortable face and decide this is my time to swoop in. "Rubes, I think we need to clean up and get ready for bed."

"Is Piper still reading to me?"

Piper opens her mouth but I shake my head. "Not tonight, bug."

"Why?"

"Because she's got stuff to do and so do we."

"We could help each other! My teacher says many hands make light work. And that means if people work together, all the work goes faster. Like how we made dinner." Ruby talks fast, gestures wildly and seems frenzied. I can tell she's a few minutes away from an exhaustion tantrum. I clench my abs.

Piper, mercifully, reaches across the table and squeezes Ruby's hand. "I might have to beg you for a rain check for that bedtime story, Ruby. I forgot I told my friend Orla I'd feed her bunny while they're out of town."

Ruby's eyes fly wide open. "You know someone with a bunny?"

Piper laughs. "Oh, man, Orla knows all the bunnies in Pittsburgh. The animal rescue is right around the corner from you and your dad. Oh, I should reach out to them about doing bunny fitness or something..." Piper reaches into her leggings and slides out her phone, tapping some notes on the screen. I try not to watch as she slides the phone back into those tight pants.

I do not succeed.

"There are bunnies around the corner?" Ruby looks between me and Piper.

I raise my hands in a *who knew* gesture. "The shelter just moved there recently."

"I want to go see."

"I will look up their hours." I've learned not to give Ruby a flat-out yes or no for these types of scenarios. Looking up the opening hours is not a commitment to anything, and

Ruby knows it. I can see the steam rising out of her ears as she prepares to mount a meltdown.

"Anyway!" Piper's voice clears the energy at the table. "I'm going to rinse my bowl. Ruby, will you show me how your dish washer works?"

Ruby giggles. "It works as a drying rack. It's broken."

"Someone should call an electrician," Piper jokes, and Ruby laughs harder.

Watching this woman make my daughter laugh is doing things to me. This goes a little beyond me checking out her body. This is...I shake my head again. Not gonna go there.

I really cannot handle this. The last time I had feelings for someone, I lost her. I cannot have a woman in my house cracking jokes with my child.

By the time I gather my wits, Piper has rinsed her plate and snuck out the back, and Ruby has gone upstairs to bed all on her own.

18

PIPER

THE AIR SEEMS TO CRACKLE AT BRIDGES AND BITTERS FOR tonight's Foof meeting. I'm not sure if that's because Esther finally turned the heat on or because the sheer force of these amazing women literally sends sparks through the air.

Juniper Jones strides into the back room like a queen, beaming because she just formalized a slew of adoptions for kids who were in the foster system like she used to be.

Nicole Kennedy-Brady dances around with her glass of Pear-ly Contained Rage, glowing because her company just had another quarter of growth.

Honestly, it should be intimidating, all these bad-ass women at the top of their game. But instead, it's the opposite. Foof cares about all of us. We redirect our fucks to the right places, as Samantha Vine likes to say.

Which is why, when Esther calls things to order by setting down a tray of drinks with a clang, I shoot my hand in the air to share the weird and wonderful developments I've got going on at Pipe Fitters.

After I get to the part about making spaghetti with Ruby, Samantha holds up a finger and purses her lips. "Let me get this straight. This red-haired burly man tried to get your business shut down, spoke to you rudely—"

"To be fair it was like five in the morning. Nobody is pleasant that early."

Samantha points her finger at me, her expression stern. "He spoke to my Piper rudely, and we haven't burned his house down? We are cavorting with him instead?"

Now it's my turn to purse my lips. Esther interjects, "I gave his friend from the city an earful. That entire department is always sniffing around in here, checking my sink drains and air vents."

Juniper winces. "It's really their job to do that, guys. Come on, now...do you *want* Piper to have to appear before my bench because someone's suing her for electrical burns? Sorry, Pipes. Actually, not sorry."

"Ugh." I toss back a swig of my drink. "It's true he was grumpy. But he sort of apologized and he's fixing the electrical for me. For free. I think..."

Sam squints.

Esther pats her on the shoulder. "Piper's gym gals have things handled, anyway. From what I hear this guy's about to get the shaft from the entire PTA at the elementary school."

All the women who have kids gasp and lean forward, riveted. Samantha gestures for Esther to continue. "They were in here the other night, Piper's clients. They're giving Sasquatch some really shitty room parent jobs and...something about a pre-dawn shift at the bake sale."

Emma Stag cackles so hard she almost falls off her chair. "Tell me they've got him chaperoning the field trip to the symphony. Please, tell me he has to straighten 20 bowties and dressy tights." Logan and Maddie join Emma in a prolonged laughing fit, muttering about karma.

Once they've caught their breath and calmed down, I ask, "how do you know about symphony field trips?"

Maddie waves a hand. "All the elementary schools do the same field trip circuit. The district gets grants for it. Anyway, you mentioned something about burly muscles?"

Esther nods. "Oh, he's got some. I saw the bubble butt."

"You guys, come on." I flush, remembering my own lingering glances on Cash's backside. I really thought I had trained myself not to notice such things. In my line of work, there are always men with no shirts, or men in spandex. I really thought I had developed a sort of professional distance, where I could appreciate a sculpted muscle and not dream about it at night. But Cash Brennan has something else going on entirely. He's...my nemesis. I have to remember that.

"So anyway..." I try to get the conversation back on track. "I need to maintain my current client roster and figure out some way to bring in a little more income while I fix up the space or, well, you know...I'm fucked."

"What about those PTA moms?" Emma, who can't drink alcohol due to her epilepsy medication, sips ginger ale with the same garnish Esther puts on our pear cocktails.

"What about them? They're my best clients."

She nods. "Exactly. I bet they can get you into the school. Do a family fitness showcase or something...strum up some more business."

"Oooh, I love that." Maddie claps her hands. "My kids climb all over me when I try to do workout videos at home. I should enroll in your classes anyway, Piper. If there was something at the school it would be such good motivation."

A chorus of agreement rises around the table and I pull out my phone to type a note to myself to text my clients later to see if anyone can make an introduction.

The conversation shifts to Chloe's new romance book release and her plans for the audiobook. "And gals, once this one is wrapped up, I think Teddy and I are going to try again to get pregnant." This announcement unleashes a torrent of celebration, which drifts to conversation about how self-employed people plan for parental leave. I tune out, daydreaming about a school gym full of parents, learning some fun ways to get their heart rate up, maybe include the kiddos or distract them enough to at least get in a set of deep squats.

I don't know where I'd be without this network. Still crying in the bathroom at the corporate gym, I guess, watching while mean men stole all my clients and treated them poorly.

As I finish typing my note to myself, my phone buzzes in my hand and I click the preview to open a message from an unknown number. It's a video of my gym, and I watch as the lights flick on and off and on again before the camera flicks to Cash Brennan nodding.

I watch the video a few more times as Chloe talks about casting narrators. Cash really fixed the lights in just a few days. I guess we're even now?

I need to call off the hounds on the PTA anyway. I suppose Foof's idea could be a nice way to get them to shift their helping energy from petty revenge to networking.

I tuck my phone back in my pocket, my thoughts wandering to all the ways I might ask Ayana and Naomi to help me make inroads with the moms at Ruby's school.

19

CASH

MY KID JUST CALLED ME USELESS. I STARE AT HER IN SHOCK, shirtless in my dress slacks and fancy shoes as Ruby yanks on her hair and screams. "You are just the most *useless* man in history. You ruin everything!"

Before I can parent this situation, she tears out the back door and into the yard, where she balls her hands into fists and releases a primal scream that will certainly wake the neighbors, if not the residents of the Homewood Cemetery a mile away.

"Ruby!" I stick my head out the back door, trying to shield my naked torso. "Get back in here right now."

"No! I want to go live with Emerald because her mom *can braid hair!*"

I blow out a breath and cling to the door. I knew this day was coming, tried to plan for it carefully. I've watched all the YouTube channels. I know what a fish tail is. How in the heck am I supposed to create a princess braid to take a second grader to the symphony? Who even knew *The Little Mermaid* was something a symphony could play for kids? All I know is we need to be at the school in about 15 minutes and I'm missing a day of paid work to chaperone this nightmare.

Before I can bodily haul my child back into the house, I see Piper, clad in her usual leggings, emerge from her bright green toy car in the alley. "Ruby! What's wrong, honey?" Piper doesn't even lock her car door before dashing over to my daughter. Piper squats in the grass and looks her square in the eye while they talk. I have a brief vision of sharing parenthood with her, of watching the two of them play in the yard while I cook dinner. Where the hell did that come from?

I hear a lot of gasping and weeping and can just make out Piper nodding in the pre-dawn autumn light. And then the two of them are headed my way, holding hands. Ruby appears to be skipping. "Piper's gonna fix it." Ruby huffs inside, slaps a brush on the table and plunks into her seat in the dining room.

Piper waves timidly and slides past me, looking like she'd rather scrape her back on the coat hooks than risk bumping into my chest. I guess that's fair since we barely know each other. I haven't even had my coffee yet, which is probably why I'm not freaking out more that I'm shirtless in front of the vexing woman who is at least fifty per cent responsible for this situation. I'm sure of it.

I stand in silence, watching as Piper picks up the brush and starts combing Ruby's hair. Ruby closes her eyes like she's getting a massage. When I brush Ruby's hair, she squirms and shrieks. I don't see anything special about Piper's brush strokes from my angle, but I pour myself a mug of caffeine so I can more accurately assess this situation.

I slurp the coffee and watch Piper's fingers bend and weave through Ruby's dark hair, forming a circular braid that clings around Ruby's head like a crown. The vision comes back, of Piper in this house, in pajamas, doing our morning routine with Ruby and me. I blink that away and lean in for the final moments, when Piper tucks in the ends and hides the hair-tie. "There," Piper says, squeezing Ruby's shoulders. "You look just like Ariel. If she had dark hair."

Ruby sighs, blissfully. "Thank you, Piper. Can I see?"

"Sure. Go look." Ruby bounds upstairs to, I assume, stare at herself in the bathroom. Piper slides her hands in the pockets of her leggings. "So. Thanks for the video of my lights."

I grunt.

"Thanks also for fixing the lights."

I slurp my coffee, nodding. And then I remember that we're late and I'm topless. "I need to get my act together. As you saw, it's been quite a morning."

Piper smiles. I should offer her coffee or smile back or something, but I just stand there. "Okay, well, I'm right back there in the alley if you have any more hair emergencies."

"Wasn't an emergency." I shake my dress shirt from where I tossed it on the table in hot pursuit of my child. I shrug into it, wishing I'd put on an undershirt, wincing at the rough material against my skin. Piper stares at me the entire time, and maybe I slow down a little as I button up. I'm not going to tuck my shirt in with her here, though. Definitely not.

She flings her own braid back over one shoulder. "Right. I'll let you get back to your field trip prep, then."

I follow her toward the door so I can lock it behind her, wondering if she ever locked her car. And then it hits me. "How'd you know about the field trip?"

She flushes. "Oh, some of my clients have kids in school with Ruby. They brought it up this morning."

I furrow my brow, not quite believing her, but she waves and skitters across the yard. I finish getting ready, stuffing myself into clothes that feel deeply unnatural, and wish I could shove a ball cap on my head. "Ready to go, Rubes?"

"Yes, Cash, I'm ready for the symphony." Ruby adjusts her tights and pats her braids.

WE DRIVE to the school and I feel the other parents staring at me at drop-off. At first I think it's just because I'm dressed differently, but I'm soon convinced there's something else going on. At least five of the boys in Ruby's class have come up to me for help with their clip-on ties and I definitely see their parents whispering to one another as I fumble with the metal clasps.

When I duck into the school bus, I assume Ruby will sit up front with me, but she skips off toward the back of the bus with her friend Emerald and when I glance out the window, I see Emerald's mom stop smiling the second we make eye contact. Something weird is going on.

And I know it's related to Piper Conklin.

THE REST of the week is more of the same, with parents at school acting super strange whenever I see them in person. And a lot of those sightings are moms leaving workout classes in the park, so now I know for certain that Piper is somehow poisoning their minds against me.

Not that I was ever Mr. Friendly to them to start with.

All of a sudden, I'm getting emails to show up at bake sales and threatening messages about classroom volunteer duties totally opposite what I signed up for at the beginning of the school year. They've got me scraping play dough from table tops, and I know that shit is full of boogers. To make it all worse, I'm losing out on sleep. Strangely, Ruby has been calmer after school and I have been able to sneak over to my studio to record a few commercial voiceover gigs, so I guess the sleep deprivation isn't a total loss.

But, as one school mom after another sniffs and looks away from me at half-day pickup, I'm about to lose my shit. And then Ruby's gym teacher comes outside grinning.

I just know someone has signed me up for something extra obnoxious.

20

CASH

I'M WEARING GYM SHORTS AT SEVEN IN THE MORNING, standing in an elementary school gym with a dozen energetic children. Ms. Bartle was overjoyed to learn that I signed up to occupy any kids who had to come along to this morning's family fitness event, so their parents could concentrate on the instructor.

The instructor is, of course, Piper Conklin, swanning around the other end of the gym with yoga mats and a smile. A group of moms huddles near her, gazing at her like she invented the iPad. Ruby swats me in the leg. "Cash, you said we'd do fun stuff. We're supposed to move our bodies."

I glance down at her. This is not my strong suit, coming up with activities. I thought Ms. Bartle would set out balls or scooters or something for us to work with. I frown at the corner closet and ask Ruby, "can you break in there and get us some equipment? Cones? Anything?"

Ruby's eyes fly wide. "We aren't allowed in there! That's for school workers only." Another child—Ruby's friend Emerald—sidles up to confirm this space is off limits.

"Well," I tell them. "I'm a deputy school worker today.

They did let me in here with you kids. So go on in and grab a few balls and cones. Hop to it."

Ruby seems unsure, but her friend seems to think this newfound permission is delightful, and soon the entire gaggle of kids is rooting around the closet. This gives me a minute to shift closer to the actual event and listen in.

"I hear those kinds of challenges all the time," Piper says, squeezing the pale arm of a mother with short, fuzzy hair and the same Pittsburgh t-shirt as me. Piper continues, saying, "We aren't here today to try out for the Olympics. We're going to learn some basic bodyweight movements you can do in short bursts of time. One of these days, I could show up for pickup and see you all outside doing some moves while you wait for the kids!"

There's a chorus of laughter before Piper starts demonstrating squats. She faces them, which means she's facing away from me, giving me a detailed view of her backside in purple tights as she rocks back on her heels, bends her knees, and thrusts her butt.

I stare too long, because a terrible crash rips my attention to the closet where I've sent the children. A few of them tumble out the door in a tidal wave of playground balls and hockey sticks. Ruby emerges from the heap with a baseball glove on her head. "Shit." I mutter the word and the children's eyes widen, like they've never heard an adult use bad language before. Maybe they haven't. I don't really hang out with of other parents.

I sigh and wade through the detritus, picking up the equipment bin and sending the children off through the gym to fetch all the Wiffle balls that rolled away. I hear the moms giggling and look over my shoulder to find them all squatting and standing as the kids crawl through their legs.

"This is great," Piper shouts. "The kids will always be

around. Trust me, I remember climbing up my own parents whenever I had the chance. But now you know a few ways to make it a game and still get your heart rate up." She rattles off a few statistics about how even a few moments of movement like this per day can improve people's health.

By the time I get the equipment closet put back to rights, Piper has everyone lying on yoga mats to work on ab movements. "Okay," she pats Ruby's arm. "So the kids can either jump on your stomach and make you mad...or you can put them to work and have them hold your feet while you crunch!" Ruby sits on Piper's feet as Piper demonstrates a reaching crunch movement. Then Piper has the kids join in a bicycle game and soon everyone in the gym is laughing and moving their feet together while I stand to the side, alone.

An outsider like always.

My dreams were too big for the neighborhood, my mistakes were too big for the college lifestyle, and now I don't fit in to this world of my kid's, either. I lean against the wall of the equipment closet as Piper continues the class, incorporating all the kids into the workout, seeming not to notice me.

AFTER CLASS, I'm tapped in to help the boys change into their school uniforms in the bathroom while entrusting Ruby's outfit change to the school moms. My calloused fingers struggle with all the buttons on all the polo shirts, but eventually I stagger into the hall with a crew of tidily dressed elementary kids ready to transition to their school day.

I locate Ruby, who is neatly tucked with her hair

braided, and she's clinging to Emerald's arm. Emerald, in turn, is clinging to the arm of her mother. "Cash!" Ruby waves me over. "Can I sleep over at Emerald's house Friday? Pleeeease? Her mom can pick us up from the half day and everything. Then you won't miss a damn gig!"

My face flushes as Ruby repeats my grumbled words to the school crowd. "Aw, Ruby, I don't know about a sleepover. We've never done that before..."

Emerald and Ruby are practically vibrating, bouncing up and down and squeezing each other. Emerald's mom smiles down at her daughter and looks up at me. "I'm Ayana," she says, extending a hand. "We haven't been properly introduced."

"Cash." I give her hand a squeeze and startle when she doesn't release mine.

"I've been thinking about you more than I ought to, and I think we misjudged you." I arch a brow, unsure why Ayana would think about me at all and who this *we* might be. She lets go of my hand. "You and Ruby are all alone in that house. If you were another mom, I'd have stepped up years ago to say you need a break."

My mouth works up and down as Ayana shakes her head and keeps talking. "We weren't meant to do this alone, raise these kids I mean. Ruby and Emerald get along just great. I don't keep guns or alcohol in my home. Your baby is safe with me. Say yes, and give yourself a break, Cash."

Ruby starts jumping, "Yes! Say yes, Cash! I'll be perfectly good and do chores at Emerald's and I won't use red words."

I swallow, seeing how excited my daughter is for this opportunity that should probably be more common. Kids have sleepovers all the time, right? How did I manage to mess this up, too? "So...you just pick her up Friday and I... come get her Saturday?"

Ayana beams. "I'll do you one better. I have class with Piper Saturday morning, so I can drop Ruby off beforehand."

Ruby and Emerald start dancing and jumping in a circle while Ayana gives me her cell and explains that all I need to pack for Ruby is a change of clothes and pajamas. By the time I've explained that my kid doesn't have any food sensitivities, the bell has rung, and everyone else has slipped away into the routine of their day.

21

PIPER

THINGS ARE LOOKING UP. NAOMI'S WIFE IS A STRUCTURAL engineer who bartered a building assessment for free classes for Naomi for a month. I hate to lose the tuition, but I picked up a few new clients after the school event last week, so it feels less scary. I even tried to make an early payment to Esther, but she shook her head and stuffed the check down my sports bra.

All that's left is for me to repair the holes in the wall and ceiling and schedule an inspection with Ben from the city office. Esther told me to mentally prepare for Ben to suddenly have months and months of schedule conflicts preventing him from coming down here in a timely manner, but I have a plan for that, too.

Sort of.

I figure, if Cash can get Ben out here to shut me down, surely there's something I can do to bribe him to give his buddy another call. I just have to figure out the right plan of action for that particular conversation.

The weather is terrible on Friday, just pouring gallons of rain, so I cancel my in-person classes and ask folks to join me online as I lead workouts from inside Pipe Fitters.

Sarah comments on the improved lighting as I show them how to incorporate a towel into their squats for some arm resistance. "Everyone has come so far," I marvel, smiling at the tiny windows on the laptop screen showing my students moving expertly through complicated exercises they were afraid to try a month ago. "I think you're all ready to add some weights once we get back in the gym."

At the mention of weights, Ayana perks up. "Show us the thrust and throw again. I liked that." I try to tell them it's not about me, that of course I can do things they can't yet, but the students all insist on a demonstration.

I roll my eyes and grab the barbell with a few bumper plates on each end. "Okay, just one set. But really pay attention to my form. The barbell is like your towel, right?"

I work through four or five squat thrusts and then drop the bar with a clatter. My students applaud and slowly sign off. I wave at them and shut the lid to my laptop, then startle when I see Cash standing in the doorway, watching me.

"You're going to chip the floor, throwing the weights like that."

I shake my head. "I'm really not. This isn't my first rodeo, you know. These plates are rubber."

He frowns and steps inside, reaching down to run a hand along my weights. "Besides," I say, "the floor mats are on order." He grunts. "What are you doing here in the middle of the day? Doesn't Ruby have a half day?"

He slides to the floor along the wall and rests his hands on his legs. "What am I doing here? I wish I knew." He fiddles with my barbell, rolling it back and forth in a small arc. "I should be cramming in extra work. I should be doing a lot of things. But I'm here, aren't I?"

I swallow thickly, realizing I can smell him when he's this close. He smells like Old Spice deodorant and generic man shampoo. I like it. "Where is Ruby?"

He grins and leans his head against the wall. "She's having her first sleepover. This is supposed to be my relaxation time, according to Ayana."

I smile. "Ah. Ayana's big about relaxation time. That's nice that you get some!"

"I guess." He makes no effort to move, even when I make a show of exaggeratedly checking my watch.

"So...I'm done working and am going to close up for the day..."

He looks up at me and then glances around the gym. Now would be a great time for me to ask him to get Ben to come out, but I don't say anything. My stomach growls loudly and I clutch at my middle. "Guess I need to go feed myself!"

I stand and grab my bag, sliding my laptop inside, surprised to see Cash has not moved. His eyes look a little wild as he slowly stands. "Let me buy you lunch."

I frown, taken aback by this change of interaction between us. "Why would you do that?"

He shrugs. "We're both alone and we need to eat."

I cross my arms over my chest. "I can pay for my own lunch. I'm not destitute."

Cash laughs and walks toward me. "Almost, though, right? Come on. I know a place."

When he opens the door I see the rain has stopped, although it's Pittsburgh, so who knows for how long. Cash starts to walk down the alley and I hate that I follow right behind him. We walk across Dallas Ave and down toward the animal shelter, turning left toward the smell of barbecue. My mouth starts to water.

Cash pushes open the door to a small cafe and I'm surprised to see it's packed full of people waiting in line. "What is this place?"

He arches a brow. "You never heard of Showcase barbecue?" I shake my head. "There's really no excuse for that, Piper." He gestures for me to step ahead of him in line and we wait as a few people in front of us receive their bags of food. I bite my lip, glancing into the buffet to see tons of foods I reserve as "for sometimes."

When it's Cash's turn to order, I stand in stunned silence as he has the server fill two trays of wings and ribs, green beans, and corn bread. My mouth waters even more as I smell the meat and Cash rests a hand on my arm. "It's her first time."

The server smiles at me, her brown skin gleaming with sweat in the warm room. "I'll give you extra sauce, then, honey." Before I can protest, Cash slips the woman some bills and snags the plastic bag of food from the counter. He starts walking back toward his house and as I follow behind, the sky opens up again.

"Hurry," he yells over his shoulder, clutching the bag of food to his chest as he starts to run in the rain. So I do. I follow and run until we're splashing through a puddle in his back yard, tripping into Cash's kitchen, heaving and trying to catch our breath.

22

CASH

I'm alone in my kitchen with a wet woman. My dick is very, very aware of this situation, and my chest heaves with the intensity of it all. I have no business doing anything with Piper, let alone objectifying her after I dragged her through a rainstorm. Maybe it's better if I objectify her. Then I'll stop having fantasies about co-parenting with her. Building some sort of life with her.

"So," she brushes a curtain of hair back from her forehead. Pieces of it fell free from her braid in our sprint. "You bought me barbecue?"

I grin and nod, setting the bag on the counter and wiping my hands on my jeans. I toss Piper a dishtowel from the oven handle and she dabs at her face while I get us some plates.

"I'm not used to free time," I explain, as if that sentence can illuminate my behavior this entire day. I should have been working. I should have been working my side hustle. I could have taken a damn nap. But instead I wandered out back to spy on Piper fucking Conklin and I don't regret it.

"So Ruby's at Ayana's house? With Emerald?" I nod and

fork a few servings of food onto each of our plates and then walk toward the dining room. Piper follows. "That's so nice. I used to have sleepovers every single weekend...well, until—"

Piper stops talking and slides into a chair at the dining room table. I arch a brow and set her plate down in front of her. "Until what?"

She waves a hand and reaches for a napkin. "Until I outgrew it."

I sit in the chair opposite her and then bump her foot with my foot by accident. We spend a few seconds readjusting our posture when my instincts keep screaming at me to lock my feet around her ankles, haul her closer to me. "So young girls outgrow the desire to sleep at friend's houses?"

Piper sighs and forks a green bean. "Oh. This is really good." She eats a few more as I dig in to the ribs. I don't prod her to continue her explanation because Showcase barbecue requires concentration and deep appreciation. But she hasn't tasted hers yet, so she says, "I wasn't able to reciprocate anymore once my mom died. Dad wasn't up to us having kids sleep over." She fidgets with her napkin and pokes at the cornbread with her fork.

"I'm really sorry you lost your mom." I set my rib down and reach out to touch her hand, but remember that mine is covered in sauce, so I just sort of wave it around in the air, awkwardly. "How old were you?"

"Twelve. It was very sudden." She eats another bite of the cornbread and looks back toward the kitchen, out the window toward her gym. "I have been so motivated to help women, mothers especially. Moms don't ever stop to take care of themselves—they put themselves last and ignore their health issues until it's too late."

I nod. "I have seen that firsthand..." I feel a lurch in my

chest, realizing that Piper has a deeper mission behind her work. She's really trying to make a difference in the world. I can't help but admire that.

She shrugs. "Pipe Fitters is about building fitness into our lives. Not a specific type of training. Not necessarily even weightlifting. Movement makes such a difference. You know?"

I'm about to answer her but she finally bites into one of her wings, slathered in extra sauce, and she lets loose a groan I feel in every nerve of my cock. I freeze, watching as she eats.

No. She doesn't eat. She savors.

"Dis is amazing." Piper talks with her mouth full, gnawing at the chicken. I laugh, only because there is no dignified way to eat ribs and wings and I feel like many women would be uncomfortable just going for it in front of a dude. Not that I'm so special. But Piper...she's into her meal here.

"Glad you like it." My voice comes out choked, and it sounds exactly like I'm trying not to come in my pants as I watch her lick the sauce from her fingers.

Eventually, I tell her, "I hadn't considered that Emerald would want to sleep here. Do you think Ruby wants that?"

Piper nods, using her cornbread to mop up extra wing sauce. "Oh, for sure. She'll probably ask you to reciprocate tomorrow. But you should say no. Once per weekend! Trust me. She'll be exhausted tomorrow."

"Once per weekend." I repeat her words as I watch her move on to the ribs. I can't decide if this was the worst or best idea I've ever had.

Piper pauses with a rib pinched between her long fingers. "What's the deal with Ruby's mom?"

I reach for my water glass and chug half of it. "She died. Before Ruby was born."

Piper furrows her brow. "How does that happen?"

I pull at my shirt collar, still damp from our run in the rain. "She got pregnant when we first started dating. I...we were in college. In Ohio." I chug another few slugs of water. "We were young, but we were gonna make a go of it. Had a plan to take turns finishing our degrees and work, all that stuff." Piper looks at me, not rushing me, not wincing, just waiting for me to continue. "Heather started getting really sick. We found out she had a kidney condition and pregnancy was—we couldn't do anything about it in Ohio. You know?" I never talk about this. But something about Piper opening up about her mom, advising me on sleepover protocol has me spilling my guts to her. And she's listening intently.

Piper's hands ball into fists, her knuckles white. She nods her head rapidly. "How long did...what happened? With Ruby?"

I blow out a big breath and spear some green beans with my fork. I can't believe I'm sharing all this drama with anyone, let alone the woman who has turned my life upside-down recently. But her face is very sincere, so I continue. "Heather went into kidney failure about six months in. It was...it was a shock." Piper sucks in a breath like a hiccup at this last statement. I fucking hate thinking about that time of my life. I swallow my beans. "She passed while they were doing an emergency cesarean, trying to save Ruby. Heather was 19."

Piper climbs out of her chair, tipping it over in her haste as she rushes around the corner of the table. She squats on the ground beside me and sets her hand on my thigh. I stare at it. "Cash, I am so, so sorry your family went through that. God, is still going through that."

My heart races as I realize that Piper isn't judging or withdrawing from all this kind of talk. Instead she's putting the pieces together, really looking at me and knowing the full picture, and I nod my head, because Piper's words are true. Ruby will always grieve the loss of her mother, and Heather's parents have been a wreck since we found out Heather was pregnant.

I exhale again. "Thank you." She squeezes my leg and I look at her, noticing a drop of barbecue sauce on the corner of her lip.

I reach out a hand to dab it away before I can think twice, and I gasp when Piper's tongue darts out to touch my finger. Both of us freeze, me with my hand cupping her cheek, her with her lips parted. I watch the tiny movements of her throat, watch the ticking vein and the way her skin moves as she breathes.

I look into her eyes, glistening with empathy. Not pity. I can tell the difference.

With the warmth of her skin in my palm, I feel emboldened. I lean forward, still cupping her face, and I kiss her.

I sigh in relief as she kisses me back.

We moan together as I rock forward out of the chair, kneeling with her on the hardwood floor. My fingers dig into her shoulders as I pull her toward me, feeling the softness of her breasts pressed against me. Her body is firm, practically vibrating with combined physical strength and emotional attention. Piper is here for this kiss as much as me, and that drives me wild.

I feel her tongue swipe between my lips, her fingers stroking my beard, tugging at my hair, exploring. And I want to be explored. God, I want this. And so much more.

My hips rock into her involuntarily and she groans, seemingly delighted. At some point, I wrap her damp braid around my fist and tug on it like a fantasy, exposing her throat, which I bite.

Her fingers dig into my chest as I do and Piper moans my name. "Yes, Cash. Yes."

She thrusts her hips to meet mine, grinds against my hard-on, and something about that motion sends me into a panic spiral. I remember how long it's been since I did this. My thoughts race back to Heather and her death.

I'm out of the moment and back in my reality, where this sort of physical intimacy leads nowhere good.

I freeze, panting, unsure what to do.

Realizing the shift, Piper straightens, balancing her hands on my shoulders, looking me straight in the eye. "We can stop. It's okay." I nod, unsure what just happened. What should happen next.

My heart races as she stands up and tugs on my hand. My body follows, until we are both standing awkwardly in my dining room.

"I better get going anyway." She squeezes my hand again, another time. A third. "Thank you for sharing with me. About Heather. Can Ruby know that I know?"

At the mention of my daughter's name, my entire reality crashes back to me. I can't make out with women in my home. I can't have a relationship and I certainly can't go around having casual sex. The consequences are too steep. Even though I know, rationally, that what happened with Heather is unlikely to repeat itself, I still can't quite let myself go there. I sink back into my chair and cross my arms.

Piper swallows and presses her lips together. "I won't say

anything. Not until you tell me it's okay. Or whatever. Thank you for lunch."

She stuns me by leaning forward and kissing my forehead before running out the back door, through my yard and across the alley in the rain.

23

PIPER

Samantha had a fight with her dad and siblings, so Chloe, Esther and I take her for pedicures to take her mind off things. And it works for me anyway, because my mind drifts all over the place. I stare at my toes in the warm, blue water, thinking about how Cash's lips felt yesterday. How warm his body felt against mine. How it felt to have that giant man listen intently as I talked about my mother and then confide in me about his daughter's origins. I want to think it was all just physical attraction...but I keep seeing his eyes as he talked to me.

Then Samantha smacks my arm. "Are you even listening? We're asking for business updates here."

"Sorry." I pull one foot from the water as the nail technician begins the arduous work of grating all the dead skin from my feet. When I get pedicures, they usually have to bust out the drill thing and grind my heels. Working out for a living has given me great thighs and rhino-hide feet.

I smile at Sam. "I think work is going well. I emailed the animal shelter about doing some bunny booty classes and then I was in the gym yesterday to lead a virtual workout since it was raining."

I remember the rain, remember sprinting with Cash into his kitchen. I must blush because Samantha squints at me and pokes the button on my massage chair, turning it off abruptly. "What did you do?"

Chloe leans forward from my other side, pulled from the bliss of her calf massage by Samantha's screech. I look back and forth between them. "I just had lunch with Cash. That's all."

Chloe taps her chin. "You had lunch together? That's unexpected."

Samantha shakes her head. "You don't casually lunch. You stare at menus and plan your macros or whatever you call it."

I throw my hands up in the air and protest. "I casually eat. Like yesterday, Cash casually stuck his head in and invited me to eat with him at a neighborhood place. Have you guys heard of Showcase barbecue? It's apparently a big deal."

Esther snorts from her chair on the other side of Sam. "You never heard of Showcase? Do you live in a suburb or something?"

I sigh and snatch the controller for my massage chair back from Sam's clutches. "It was delicious and I regret all the many years of not working those ribs into my some-times-food rotation."

Chloe pokes my hand on the arm of the chair. "Something doesn't add up. What did you and Cash-quatch talk about?"

"Oh, Chlo, that's good. Cash-quatch!" Esther mimes giving a high five and Chloe pretends the air-five was a kiss, catching it and blowing one back to Esther.

I switch out my feet as the nail tech fires up the grinder for my heel callouses. "He told me about Ruby's mom...she died. It's so sad."

Esther shakes a finger at me. "Piper Conklin, what do I always say? We do not try to fix sad men. This is my professional advice as a bartender."

I nod. I've heard this from Esther before. Loads of times. Women are always trying to fix sad men...and I can sort of see why. "He's just so...lonely isn't the right word. I think he built one of those mean shells to hide his damage." I nod to my own assessment of Cash. "I can relate."

Samantha repeats Esther's mantra to me. "Piper, we do not try to fix sad men. You're not going to fix him, right? You know this?"

"I don't want to fix him." The nail tech pushes a button on the electric grater thing and it roars, so I feel brave muttering, "I just want to maybe fuck him a little bit."

Samantha squeals. "Piper! I heard that! I heard what you said." She turns to Esther. "She boned the Sasquatch. I know it."

The whirring sound stops and the tech starts rubbing lotion into my heels. "We did not *bone*. I told you, there were ribs involved."

Esther frowns. "Just be careful, Piper. You've got a lot at stake here, right? Your hopes and dreams to honor your mother's legacy?"

I sink into the chair with a groan, wondering why she doesn't emphasize the fact that I also owe her thousands of dollars. "You don't need to remind me of my *why* for Pipe Fitters. And besides, I've already experienced what it's like to be on Cash's bad side. Might as well enjoy myself if he's going to eventually try to sabotage me."

Chloe grins wickedly. "Oh, so you enjoyed the ribs? Was

there any of that messy sauce?" The girls all laugh as our romance novelist friend uses her sexiest voice to make euphemisms about my lunch.

Eventually, Samantha concedes, "He does seem delightfully hairy from what I've managed to find online." She rests her head back on the chair. "There's just something bout a hairy pelt that does it for me."

"Mm," I agree, wiggling my toes to admire the new bright red polish. I'm about to elaborate when Chloe lets out a string of profanity. "What's wrong?"

She swears a few more times and slaps the arms of her massage chair. "I don't believe this. My fucking narrator just fucking quit. Again. God, this guy's such a diva."

She moans and starts rocking back and forth in her chair. As an independently-published author, Chloe handles all the aspects of her books herself, from writing and creating the covers to hiring the narrators for her audiobooks. I love following along as she brings her ideas to the page. I especially like listening to her steamy audiobooks because, well, her narrators make the whole experience really enjoyable.

"What does that mean, he quit? Don't you have a contract?"

Chloe rolls her eyes. "Yeah, he doesn't care about the money. Some bullshit nonsense about exploring other avenues for his career at this time. He's walking. I'm so fucked. I have deadlines!"

Esther, who is finished with her pedicure, waddles over to Chloe's chair with cotton twists between her toes. "Chlo, we're here with you. Let's brainstorm solutions."

Samantha nods, smiling, as my thoughts drift back to my afternoon with Cash, kissing Cash...and then I remember something. He has a garage full of recording equipment and Ruby said he does "voice stuff."

I whip my head to face Chloe. "I have an idea where you could find someone."

Chloe just stares at me and Esther says, "Don't hold back on us, Pipes. Spit it out."

I bite my lip. They're still not entirely done giving me shit about my confusing interactions with Cash to date. "The guy in the alley...he does voice stuff."

"Cash-quatch? Are we back to him already?" Samantha slips her feet into the flat nail salon flip-flops and then heaves herself out of the pedicure chair.

I look down at my own feet and see that I'm cottoned up and ready to go, too. So I climb down and waddle over to the little foot fans. "He has a garage full of professional sound equipment. I don't know what all he does out there, but I'm saying he's a possible solution to explore." Samantha opens her mouth to shut this idea down again, but I hold up a hand. "Don't you always say we shouldn't bring an umbrella to a brainstorm? I think we should check Cash out." Sam's eyes widen. I blush. I mean his work."

Esther smiles and Chloe flaps her hands a few times. "Fine. Whatever. How do I get in touch with him?"

I wiggle my toes as best I can with the cotton wedged in between them. "I think we should go over there and ambush him. He's not good on the phone."

24

CASH

Someone is knocking on my back door. Who knocks on the back door?

I'm about an hour in to fighting with Ruby about her homework, and her crabby mood has me feeling glad I said no when she asked me to stay at Emerald's house for another night. Piper got the exhaustion aspect right, that's for sure.

Piper...I feel a lump in my throat just thinking of what happened between us yesterday. I wanted so much more, and yet I was terrified of what did happen. What must she think of me?

There's another knock at the door, followed by a shout from a voice I don't recognize. "Hang tight, Rubes." My intention is to check the door while my daughter stays in the dining room in case it's about to be an unpleasant interaction, but she follows right behind me.

"It's Piper!" Ruby dashes ahead and flings open the door to reveal Piper Conklin standing on my porch. Holding a pie. Surrounded by elegant women.

"Hey, Ruby!" Piper smiles and wiggles some fingers,

balancing the pie, which smells like it's a freshly baked apple variety.

"What do you want?" My question comes out harsher than intended, but I just spent an hour arguing about subtraction facts and, after all, these women approached my house from the back. It's all very strange.

Piper thrusts the pie toward me. "We have a proposition for you and we're hoping we could come in to discuss it."

I stare at the pie, still confused about this disruption in my day, when one of the women with dark hair shoves her way to the front of the group. "We need a voice actor, and we can pay." She grabs the pie from Piper and hands it to Ruby, who licks her lips and weaves her way around my legs to put the steaming pastry on the counter.

"Voice actor?" The hairs on my arms stand up at the idea that Piper has somehow come across my side hustle. She must really know every one of my secrets now.

"We're coming in," says the blonde one, giving Piper a shove that sends her stumbling into my chest. I put my hands on her elbows to catch her, feeling a swoop in my gut at the sensation of being close to her again. I release her and take a step back as the women file inside.

"You must be Ruby," the blonde one says, offering a hand to my kid, who shakes it. "I'm Samantha Vine. Will you show me your living room?"

Ruby skips off as Piper and the other two women make themselves comfortable in my dining room. "Okay," Piper says, "This is my friend Chloe Preston, but her professional name is Chloe Petals and she's kind of a big deal."

"Hi!" Chloe waves. Piper charges on, explaining that Ruby showed her all my recording equipment when I was fixing the electrical in Pipe Fitters and they're here because they need me to do some "voice stuff."

My jaw drops. I can't help but show my surprise. "Ruby told you?"

Chloe winces. "I'm sorry if your stage name is outed or something. I swear I will not tell a soul your identity. But your samples are amazing and I can hear from your voice right now that you'd be perfect."

Piper nods. "And Chloe's in a tight spot! And you've already got all the stuff in your garage, so..."

I cross my arms over my chest, leaning against the built-ins skeptically. "You think I want to be in my garage recording at five in the morning?"

Piper's eyebrows shoot up. "Is that what you do out there when I'm trying to teach?"

I roll my eyes. "It's what I *was* doing out there before you invaded the neighborhood. You kept ruining my shit with your background noise. I almost lost a contract over it." It should feel more shocking that these women know about my side hustle, that they now see me as something other than a dad and an electrician. But there's something about Piper Conklin that makes it feel safe somehow, to just part the curtains and be me.

She winces but pats Chloe on the back. Ruby hollers from the living room that I'm being too loud and she can't hear Kid Bop.

Piper furrows her brow. "Why do it at the crack of dawn, though? Why not wait until Ruby goes to school?"

I drum my fingers along the bookshelf at my side, trying to remain calm. "I wouldn't think I'd need to explain to you that I need things like health insurance and money for a mortgage."

The dark-haired woman stands and says she's going to serve the pie. Chloe folds her hands and leans toward me. "Cash, I'm in a tight spot. I have a 120,000 word historical romance novel publishing in three weeks and my narrator up and quit. I need the audio files as soon as humanly possible. I looked you up on the way here and listened to your reel—I pay union rates and can do a rush fee."

My body melts a little bit in surprise. I never even considered audiobook narration as an option. The guys who do that seem like actual pros, not garage amateurs like me. And union rates? I never joined the voice actors union because I didn't think I'd be able to land the jobs that paid those wages. Some quick mental math leaves me dizzy with the possibilities. Chloe looks over her shoulder. "Oh, here's Esther with the pie. Why don't you sit and ask us any questions you might have."

Esther—the dark-haired one—sets a slice of pie at my place at the head of the table. I make my way toward the seat, grateful my body isn't shaking on the outside. I robotically take a bite and then groan. "This is really good."

Piper beams. "It's grain free and vegan and sweetened with monk fruit! It's great for my clients working through diabetes."

I keep chewing, not wanting to think about a pie that tastes this good, made from whatever pretend ingredients she found to eliminate the butter and stuff that usually makes pie taste like pie. The filling is silky and warm, and damn it, now I'm thinking about her skin feeling the same way under my tongue.

"So anyway," Piper takes a bite of her own pie and swallows it. "The plan is that I can hang out with Ruby while you work on Chloe's book recording. We'll just have to map out a schedule to avoid conflicts with my classes, but the other Foof gals can also step in if it means getting the book sooner."

I swallow without properly chewing. "Floof?"

Esther waves a hand. "Foof. It's a long story. Just trust us. We've got Ruby taken care of."

"Why would I trust people I never met with the care and keeping of my only child?" I lean back in my chair and cross my arms again.

Esther shrugs. "You trusted Piper..." She taps her chin. "Or...wait...Piper stepped up to help you without asking, didn't she? Something about an unattended child in a park..."

Piper blushes and I drop my hands to the arms of my chair, white knuckling the wood. Esther pats the tabletop. "We need our gal Chloe to meet her deadlines. Let's work out a deal here."

I stare at Piper. "What's in it for you?"

"For me? What do you mean?" She looks genuinely confused by the question.

"Why would you do something like this for someone else? Babysit my kid...offer me a gig...I treated you like shit."

She tucks her stray hair behind her ears and looks back and forth between her friends. "These are my friends and Chloe needs help. They'd do it for me."

I arch a brow. "I didn't see them here when your business got shut down."

Piper's eyes fly wide and I think I see a flame fly out of one of her pupils. "What do you mean? Esther *was* here when your jerky friend shut me down. And Foof helped all my clients wage some sort of petty PTA war against you. I had nothing to do with that, by the way."

Esther snorts. "I hear you had to tie about a hundred tiny bowties at the symphony."

I glare at her. "You were responsible for that? Why would I help you, knowing you made me chaperone a field trip? Do you know how long it took me to get those kids across the street downtown? I almost got mowed down by a scooter."

Samantha reappears in the doorway. "The way I see it, the field trip was payback for the building inspector. The electrical repair was payback for the initial babysitting. You two are even, but you're going to take this gig because I know you want it."

Samantha points to a framed photo on the shelf in my dining room, a picture of me taking my bow from the one stage production I got to complete while I was in college. My parents had driven to Ohio to watch. That was the night I got Heather pregnant...

My face softens, remembering how she told me she wanted me to be able to keep up with my dreams. Ruby's been my only focus for a long time. What would it even feel like to perform again—not just a commercial or public service announcement, but an entire manuscript...

I look at my daughter, who is standing on the couch dancing and beaming at Samantha, who is apparently her best friend after ten minutes of hang time. I look back at Chloe and sigh. "What sort of romance novel are we talking about here?"

25

CASH

Piper shows up at my house Sunday afternoon, right on schedule. She's dressed the same as always: workout gear, Converse sneakers, long hair tied back in a variety of braids. She looks a bit like a Viking warrior when she smiles at Ruby and asks if she's ready to bounce.

In this case, Piper means that literally. She's taking Ruby to a trampoline park, which is apparently a thing that exists. Over the years, Ruby has had a few invitations to birthday parties at these sorts of places, but they're all in the suburbs and I could never get it together to haul her out that far for a 90-minute party.

Based on the look in my daughter's eyes, she has definitely felt the loss. She wrings her hands together and tugs at her own braids. "Do I look okay, do you think? Cash did the pigtails."

Piper waves off the concern. "You look perfect. Nice, sensible bottom layer that won't reveal your undies as we do tricks."

Ruby's mouth falls open. "You're going to jump with me?"

Piper's laugh is a tinkling sound, and it fills the room with light. "Of course I'm going to jump. I've even got some Pipe Fitters students meeting me there for a workout. Maybe you've heard of Emerald's mom? And Zack's mom?"

"Emerald and Zack are gonna be there, too? Yes!" Ruby bounces and claps her hands and bolts out the front door. "Where's your car? Can we go now?"

Piper blocks Ruby's exit from the porch and asks me, "Anything I need to know? Allergies? Food aversions? You signed that waiver I texted you?"

I nod, and then realize that's not the right answer to some of those questions. "Ruby's good with all the foods. You're the one who gets her to eat vegetables...and yes, I signed my life away."

Piper shoots finger guns at me. "Perfect. See you in four hours!" I watch as she bends to help Ruby into the back seat of the clown car. The two of them wave and Piper meeps the tiny horn as they zoom away.

And then it's just me, an afternoon, and the best-paying gig I've ever had in my life. And that's saying something, because electricians earn pretty good money. But I don't have to give a cut of this to my dad or anyone else's company.

I just need to read this damn book to get a feel for the role I'm playing. The version of the manuscript Chloe sent me seems pretty well annotated. It's obvious she's worked with narrators before, because she has all sorts of margin notes about how the hero is supposed to have a gruff voice and he's often short-tempered and abrupt when he talks to the heroine.

Well, that won't be too much of a stretch for me.

I skim through the first few chapters before I find myself really caught up in the part where Patrick is called up to fight with the Pittsburgh Blues in the War of 1812. I thought this book was going to be some fluffy love story, but here I am biting my nails to see if Patrick is going to have to leave behind his life as a shopkeeper, where he supports his parents and widowed sister and her children.

"This guy has the weight of the world on his shoulders," I mutter, making a note to keep the tone pretty serious.

Ruby's bird clock starts tweeting like crazy and I see it's somehow noon, and that I've been reading this book for two hours. I have to at least get a few character voice tracks in the can, and I rush out to the garage, still feeling the adrenaline rush of empathy for Patrick's situation.

After a brief warmup and a mouth full of green apple to prevent slurping sounds from my spit, I slide into the headphones, click on the recording equipment, and just begin.

"'They called us volunteers,' Patrick McLintock scoffed as he showed the parchment to his sister. The tattered sheet was deeply creased and spattered with something, and Patrick wasn't altogether certain it wasn't the saliva of his fellow conscripted militiamen."

THE SOUND of a metal garage door rolling up snaps me out of my groove and I notice that I've been performing for an hour. I didn't even remember to stop the track at the end of the chapter, to separate the files like Chloe requested. I can take care of all that in post-production, but what stuns me is the trance I've been in.

Rather than clenching my entire body, waiting for my kid to burst into the garage, I've just been deep inside this character, this story. I'm almost tingling with the energy of it all. I stare at the equipment and swallow thickly. I take a few breaths in the stillness of my little booth, where I just got to spend the day honing my craft.

That's a phrase my teachers used to use at college. It's been a long time since I've thought about terms like *craft.*

I carefully hang my headphones up and make sure all my files saved before I open my own garage door to see if the sound came from Piper in the alley, hopefully with my kid in tow. It surprises me how comfortable and relaxed I felt while Ruby was off with Piper, but I didn't worry about her welfare at all this entire time.

I can't help the smile that almost cracks my face when I see the two of them. Ruby looks sweaty and delighted, sitting on a rubber tire with Piper, the two of them sipping sports drinks and laughing.

My heart surges a little before I realize this is all just temporary. This isn't my little girl getting a sense of what it could be like to have a mother. This is my neighbor looking after my daughter for me while I'm working. Piper is doing this to be nice. She's not on board for our baggage. I need to have a talk with Ruby about getting too attached. We can't expect these hang sessions with Piper to go on indefinitely. She has a whole mission-driven career taking her places, and Ruby and I go to bed at eight each night.

This is exactly why I need to stop reminiscing about that ill-advised kiss in my dining room. No good can come of any of that.

The two of them look up and Piper shields her eyes from the sun as she waves. "Hey! Did you get a lot done?"

Ruby bounds across the alley, babbling about special grippy socks and doing a zip line into a foam pit. "That all sounds very tiring."

She clings to my leg and shakes her head. "I am not tired. That was the best day ever."

"Yeah? You want to tell me more about it inside?" She nods and runs toward the house, stops in her tracks, and spins around before running back and crashing into Piper.

"Thank you thank you thank you, Piper."

"Thank *you* for being the best ninja warrior teammate ever. Make sure to tell your dad how we dominated the championship."

Ruby grins and grabs my hand to tug me inside. "Just a second, kiddo. Let me say goodbye to Piper." I swear, my tiny child rolls her eyes at me, even though she's way too young to be doing that sort of thing.

I rub a hand on the back of my neck awkwardly and smile at Piper. "What do I owe you for the park admission?"

She waves a hand. "Nothing. I made bank today leading a parent-kid fitness session at the trampoline place *and* Ruby told at least ten other parents about how I work to keep all the moms healthy. I gave out my entire business card stash." Her smile is—there's no other word to describe this—breathtaking.

I'm actually short on oxygen as I look at Piper, whose face is flushed and glowing from exercise. Her entire body seems happy, and I realize she's not faking any of it. She just exudes joy.

I clear my throat. "Well, I really appreciate it. I got a lot done today."

"Oh, good. Chloe is going to be able to relax a little! Can I hear a sample?" She wags her eyebrows and I block her from entering the garage.

"Um, it's all very much a rough draft at this point. I don't think I should share any of it. I signed a non-disclosure and stuff..."

Piper nods, her face wide with surprise. "I should have known Chloe would take the whole thing very seriously."

She grins. "I'll just have to wait with the rest of the world. I'm dying to see who Chloe pairs Patrick with. He was such a fun side character in her last book…"

I want to invite her inside to sit on the couch with me as I read aloud from the manuscript. I want to summarize the whole thing to her and watch her facial expressions as I reveal each point of the plot. But none of that fits into the life Ruby and I have right now. None of that is sustainable.

And so I hook a thumb over my shoulder. "I gotta get inside to Ruby. So…"

Piper sucks in a breath and holds up her hands. "Right. Of course. I will talk to you soon, okay? You still need to send me your ideal schedule so I can compare with my classes and stuff."

With a promise to do that later this evening, I shut my garage door, rolling a literal barrier between me and this woman who does unwelcome things to my carefully constructed life.

26

PIPER

As it turns out, Ruby Brennan is good for business. My business, anyway. Today after school, she asked her dad again about going to the animal shelter and I remembered my to-do list item about asking to host a fitness class there as a fundraiser.

Ruby actually skips down the sidewalk as we head to the shelter, and I almost feel joyful enough to skip alongside her. We arrive just in time for their "animal tales" volunteer event, where kids can grab a book and go read to the dogs and cats. Ruby, of course, wants to read to the rabbits.

"You're practically writing my business plan for me," I whisper as she tugs my hand down the hall to the room with the rabbit pens. She looks at me like I'm nuts and I wave a hand, dismissively. Ruby plunks onto the floor next to a bonded pair of angoras and starts reading them a book about trains. I lean against the wall, smiling, until a staff member approaches to change the rabbits' hay.

"Hey," I say, groaning inwardly at the pun they must hear constantly.

"Hey," the volunteer responds with a wink. She's a short woman with a trendy haircut and a puffy sweater covered in bits of hay.

Ruby continues to read, undeterred by my stuttering sales pitch. I bite my lip and then just go for it, saying, "Do you guys ever host fitness classes with the rabbits? As fundraisers?"

"Like goat yoga?" The volunteer pauses, considering. "We've done that at our wildlife rescue location in the past. I'm not sure about rabbit yoga."

"I was thinking like a bunny booty camp sort of thing." I reach into my pocket for a business card. "I own a gym around the corner. Pipe Fitters. I'd love to talk with someone about a collaboration?"

The staffer smiles and hands my card back to me. "You're in luck. Our outreach coordinator is here tonight to supervise the reading program." She nods her head down the hall. "Third door on the left."

I look down at Ruby, who is sounding out words and making train sounds for the rabbits, who seem genuinely invested in the story. "I'll just be down the hall for a few minutes, okay, Ruby?" She nods her head and turns the page. I know Cash keeps a pretty close eye on her usually, but the building is crawling with volunteers and kids reading to cats, so I feel okay walking a few doors down the hall to do some networking.

I tap on the door frame of the third office, as suggested, and a young guy looks up from a cluttered desktop where a plaque informs me he's named Ronin. "Yes?"

"Hi, I'm Piper. I own the Pipe Fitters gym around the corner." I repeat my spiel and watch as his face lights up.

"We just finished renovating our event space," he says.

"This could be a great idea. I want to make sure you understand how the rabbits behave, though, to avoid any confusion." He explains how rabbits are prey animals and won't be as relaxed around people as goats. "They wouldn't want to hop all over the participants. But we could have them in some low exercise pens around the room. No loud music for the class..."

Ronin ticks off parameters and I pull up a chair, responding to his questions with ideas for the class. "I sort of love that you have a lot of rabbits with health conditions. I am so passionate about helping humans avoid preventable health conditions!"

He spins his monitor toward me and we look at some dates. "This is a cool idea," Ronin grins. "What brought you in tonight to suggest it?"

I remember that Ruby has been unattended for a bit now and I gasp. "Oh my gosh. My...friend...is reading to the rabbits. I have to go check on her." I dash out the room and down the hall in a mild panic, but find Ruby almost exactly where I left her.

I see that Ronin has followed me and he smiles as Ruby turns to read her book to a group of lop-eared bunnies who, again, seem really interested in the story. "I'm so glad someone is reading to these guys. They get looked over a lot. Along with the rats."

Ruby snaps her head up to look at Ronin. "You guys have rats?"

He grins. "Oh yeah. We have a whole room of small mammals. Want to see?" She leaps to her feet and turns abruptly back to the bunnies.

"Sorry, guys. I'll be back later. Maybe."

She dashes down the hall after Ronin and I follow, grinning and floating. Apart from the whole "reported me to the city" situation, I have to say things are turning into a net positive for me and my involvement with the Brennan household. Ronin tells Ruby all about the resident guinea pigs as I fantasize about the hoards of new clients I can pick up hosting classes here.

Even if I just get two more regulars, I'll hit my "comfortable" threshold for income at the gym, where comfortable is just enough past break-even that I don't have to cancel my health insurance. Easy street is where I can start making regular payments to Esther. A voice comes over the loudspeaker announcing the end of the volunteer event and Ruby frowns.

"No worries, pal." I set a hand on her shoulder. "We'll definitely be back. Mr. Ronin and I are organizing a class here."

"I want to take it." Ruby puts her hands on her hips, assertively.

I smile at Ronin. "Thoughts on doing it family-style instead of just for adults?"

He winces ever so slightly. "That's a complicated question. Kids are prone to impulsive movements. Might not be the best fit for a class with rabbits...but we could think about cats..."

I sigh and nod. "I'm pretty committed to the alliteration of bunny booty camp. Ruby, maybe we could just make a plan to come regularly for animal tales?"

She shakes her head. "I want to take the bunny class with Cash. Please?"

Ronin holds his hands up. "I'll let you two navigate this roadblock." He smiles and reaches in his pocket for the card I gave him. "I will be in touch to finalize, though. Thanks, Piper."

As he walks down the hall and other families file past us

to leave, Ruby grows increasingly agitated. "It has to be the bunny class. Didn't you see how good I was with the rabbits?"

I reach for her hand but she snatches it back. I start to walk down the hall and try to simultaneously move and calm her. "I did see that. I think they have general rules here, though, because of statistics."

"What's that mean?"

I push open the door to the shelter and feel relief when she walks through it ahead of me. "It means *most* kids make the kinds of jerky movements Ronin was describing. Not all, but most. And they can't risk the rabbits getting upset."

"It's dumb to punish everyone if some kids can't behave."

"Yeah, that is a bummer." I remember having these sorts of arguments with my parents. Not about rabbit yoga classes, but wanting to try out for more competitive sports teams. I have this visceral memory of my mom putting her foot down, insisting that the age limitations were firm. I remember feeling betrayed just like Ruby is now. I see so much of myself in this kid.

I flash to a memory of Cash and his mouth on mine, his hands on my body, and I remember that Cash comes as a package deal. Is that even something I can do? I'm not doing so great keeping her happy at the moment. I rack my brains for a compromise.

"Tell you what." She agrees to clasp my hand as we cross the alley behind the shelter, heading up the hill toward Ruby and Cash's house. "Why don't we ask your dad about you guys adopting a pet? Then I could do a workout with you and your pet could attend and we'd all know the pet would be safe."

"Ooh. I want a rat. I want one of the rats from the shelter." The look on her face makes me happy for about an instant before I realize what I've done. I suspect Cash is going to kill me for planting this seed, and I'm surprised by how strongly I react to that possibility.

27

CASH

I TEXT PIPER THE QUESTION SINCERELY AFTER SPENDING OVER an hour trying to calm Ruby down enough to get her to sleep. What on earth could that woman have been thinking suggesting a pet for our house without asking me first? Ruby's not the kid you can just casually suggest something and then wait for her to get distracted by her brother or something.

There is no brother.

I groan and sink into the couch, exhausted. These long days are killing me, between busy season at work and putting in so much evening time recording this book for Chloe.

This fucking book. *Forking.*

I actually had to build wank time in to my plans for recording. I've been leaving the booth painfully hard, practically unable to walk after I record some of Chloe's scenes. But the thing is, none of them are gratuitous or porn-y.

It's all super emotional and hot as hell, all at the same time. Patrick knows how to treat a lady, that's for sure.

My phone buzzes on the couch, a message back from Piper.

PIPER:

??

I growl at the phone, certain she's being coy. How would Piper know any different? She's like everyone else my age without kids...no idea how tightly they hold on every word adults say. Hell—heck, I've been having to train myself not to even curse in my thoughts.

[rat emoji] [knife emoji] [angry face emoji]

The phone vibrates in my hand immediately, an incoming call from the devil herself. "Ungh." I grunt at her, the only words I feel capable of between my horny exhaustion and my frustration about the rat situation.

"Cash, I'm so sorry about the pet thing. I meant to mention it to you, but then Ruby skipped off inside and you sort of shut the door in my face and that was the end of our evening together..."

Well, shoot. She's right. I didn't really give her an opportunity to debrief. "Well," I tell her. "What I'm saying is you owe me again. I just spent an hour explaining that you have no idea what you're talking about because we are, under no circumstances, ever, getting a pet rat."

"They're actually really clean animals. Did Ruby tell you about Ronin from the shelter? He gave us a whole tour of the rodents and explained everything."

"You let some man butter up my kid and get her all

pumped about a pet rat?" Who the hell is Ronin and did he touch Piper in any way? And why the hell am I letting my mind go there? What do I care if Piper touches some other dude? A growl comes out of my throat and through the phone, and I hear Piper's sharp inhale.

"He's not *some man*. He's the outreach coordinator at the shelter. And I only suggested Ruby ask you about a pet because she was getting super upset that she can't attend my exercise class due to age requirements."

"Oh, trust me, I heard all about that, too." I sigh and drop my head against the back of the couch. "Ruby gets intense sometimes."

"I'm figuring that out." She's silent for a minute, but I start to imagine that she's here, sitting with me on the couch, reaching a hand out to stroke my arm in comfort. Maybe tapping in to soothe Ruby during another one of these situations. What in the holy fuck is wrong with me? I blame Chloe's book. But then, Piper says, "Should I come over and talk this through? I'm still in the gym." I swallow, a thick knot building in my throat. I should probably drink hot tea with honey, preserve my voice for tomorrow. But now that I think about it, I'm recording some intense scenes next and it's okay if I sound a little gravelly. "Cash? What do you think?"

I never answered Piper out loud. My hands shake a little at the thought of saying yes, because I know if she comes over here, there's no way that I will keep my mouth off hers. "Yeah," I practically whisper. "You can come in."

I hang up and throw the phone next to me, crossing my arms and staring through the living room into the kitchen, and beyond to the back door I know will open any second and reveal Piper Conklin. I have no plan in place to introduce Ruby to the idea of me dating someone. I don't even know how to date someone. I was a teenager the last time I tried that.

All I know is a woman is coming over. And I'm going to kiss her. An eternity passes before I hear the quiet click of knob and hinges.

"Cash?" Her voice is quiet, like she knows not to wake Ruby. I appreciate that. Not enough to get up from the couch, however, because I'm having another crotch situation.

She appears in the dining room and smiles when she sees me. Piper Conklin smiles when she sees *me*. "Hey," is what I manage to say in response. Because what else is there to say? *You infuriate me and fascinate me and I don't understand anything about you but I can't get enough* seems creepy.

She walks over and sits next to me and all I smell is her, fruity and soapy despite hours in the animal shelter, let alone exercising all day for a living. I wonder if she tastes like salt.

"So." She turns sideways and folds her long legs up into a pretzel, propping her elbows on her knees. "What's off limits with Ruby? Talk of her mother and pets. What else?"

I purse my lips, considering. "Trips. Pierced ears. She's asking about that a lot lately and I'm not taking her to the mall where some kid comes at her with a hole punch."

Piper laughs and relaxes back into the couch, lounging on the arm and extending her legs a bit. Her toes are an inch from my thigh. I wonder where she took off her shoes and why she doesn't smell like sweaty feet.

"I will discourage all body modifications, travel, and future animal encounters." Piper sighs and stretches and I clench all my muscles in an effort not to explode at the sight of her belly skin. I breathe slowly through my nose, trying to get a handle on myself. I feel like a horny teenager, and I spend plenty of time sitting with the ripple effects of all that youthful energy. I wonder if she's going to bring up the kiss.

"Mmm," Piper says. "Your house is really cozy. My apartment is so barren. I'm hardly ever there."

"Cozy?" I look around at the mismatched thrifted furniture and slat blinds that were hanging in the front window when I bought the house. The walls are decorated with Ruby's artwork tacked up with blue painter's tape.

"Totally cozy. It's such an obvious family space. I love it."

My eyebrows raise and I adjust my posture very carefully, risking turning toward her without drawing attention to the crotch of my jeans. "Thank you, I guess. Ruby is in charge of decor." She said family...that she loves the idea of family. I swallow, a lump in my throat.

Piper smiles and then her face grows wistful. "My mom used to let me and my brother hang our artwork, too. We had a wire Dad strung up and we used clothes pins and cycled through our drawings." She blinks a few times. "The wires are still up, but they're empty now, at Dad's house. It's kind of sad."

I nod. "Sounds definitely sad." I twist to look at the latest installment flapping in the breeze near the cracks around the front door. "We usually send stuff to Heather's parents every few weeks. We use the painter's tape so it peels off without ripping. Not that Ruby ever takes her time peeling it."

We both chuckle and then lapse into a silence that feels anticipatory. Like we're both waiting for the other to make a move. I swallow. "I really appreciate you hanging out with Ruby. Apart from the pet fiasco."

She reaches out and squeezes my arm, her skin like a brand on mine. "It's my pleasure. She's a great kid."

Piper retracts her hand and I feel cool in its absence. I swallow again, my heart starting to race in my chest. I want this woman. I know it's a terrible idea, but I know I'm going to kiss her anyway. "Piper."

She presses her lips together and raises her brows, leaning forward just the tiniest bit. The small movement pulls a trigger inside me and I lunge for her, wrapping a palm around the back of her head, sinking my mouth against hers.

An instant later, she's kneeling on my leg, her knees pressing into my thighs as her breasts rub against my arm. It feels so god damned good I moan out loud.

"Sshhh," she whispers against my lips.

I nod, continuing to kiss her. I'm as turned on by the thought of her wanting a family as I am by her body, by her touch. Like last time, her hands are all over me, exploring my hair and my beard and tickling light touches along my shoulders. By contrast, I feel like a brute, squeezing her against my face, digging my hand into her firm thigh. But then she moans into my mouth and says my name, and I hoist her fully onto my lap.

Her eyes widen as she becomes aware of my hard-on and all I can do is nod in acknowledgement. Piper tilts her hips, rocking herself against my cock and we groan in unison. "Cash." She bites my nose. "You feel so good."

"Oh, fuck, Piper." I tug at her hair and bend her head back, sucking at her neck again. She reaches under my shirt and begins to rub my stomach, reaches higher and palms my chest. I take it as a sign that she's into the same treatment and she groans quietly when I reach inside her top.

"I think about you too much," I tell her, pulling my head

apart from hers just long enough to toss the shirt up and over her head. I stare at her on my lap, at her nipples hard as cherry pits poking through her sports bra. We kiss some more as I reach for those buds with my thumbs and I feel her melt against me as I pinch and stroke. She's so sensitive, so responsive. I marvel that it's me pulling these feelings from her. We're making this pleasure together.

Piper rocks against me with intention, chasing pleasure against the ridge of my cock, and I love that I drive her mad this way, the way she makes me lose all my good sense. It's thrilling. I'm surrounded by her scent and I can't get enough of how this feels.

"God, Cash, you're so sexy." Piper tugs at my shirt and it snags against my chin as she yanks it off. I laugh at the pout on her face as she struggles to get it over my head. Then she reaches for her bra and peels it off gracefully, so quick it doesn't occur to me to help her.

"That's better," she sighs, leaning against me, nipples dragging along my chest.

"Fuuck." I drop my head back against the couch, needing to catch my breath, but she takes that as an invitation to bite my neck and that elicits a feral response from me.

I flip us over so she's on her back with those thighs wrapped around my waist. I can't wait a second longer. I have to lick her belly. I trace my middle finger from her sternum down to her waist band and follow the path with my tongue. Jesus, she tastes good. She writhes beneath me, bites her own finger to keep herself quiet.

Once I start licking that skin, I can't stop, so I don't. I make my way to her waist and meet her eyes, hooded with pupils blown. "Yes, Cash, please," she pants. So I tug at her leggings, easing them over the lush curve of her ass and realize she's not wearing any underwear.

"What in the holy fuck is this?" I glance down at her bare pussy, glistening on my couch, with no underwear. No fucking underwear. She's been on my lap with nothing but a millimeter of lycra between us.

Piper grins and then grabs my hand, bringing it to her center, pressing me against her as she tilts her hips up. "Please. Please, Cash."

She doesn't need to beg me. God, I want to make her feel good. I circle my thumb where she directs me, using my other fingers to explore the rest of her folds. She's wet and soft and hot and her thighs open for me, despite the awkwardness of the couch. I hitch my arm under one of her knees, drawing it up higher so I have more room to work, and then I bow my head and worship Piper Conklin with my mouth.

The scent of her drives me insane, raw and salty. I feel her fingers digging into my hair as I go to town, stroking and licking, delighting in the response I'm drawing from her body. I feel like king of the world as I make her moan, as she bites her lip to avoid shouting at the work I'm doing down here.

But it's not work at all. This is the best thing I've done in years, and it's totally different from any of my previous experiences. Because now I'm with her.

"Piper," I whisper, using my nose to nudge at her clit, which makes her jerk her hips and I laugh. "You're so fucking beautiful." I stop licking at her so I can watch her as I stroke her. I reach two fingers inside her and she starts to fuck herself on my hand. It's all I can do not to reach in my own pants while she gets herself off.

"I want to touch you," she whimpers. "Please?"

I nod and kiss my way up her body, unbuckling my jeans with one hand as I use the other to massage her breast. She shoves a greedy hand down the front of my pants, but I still her with a light touch to her wrist. "I need you to come first."

She stiffens. "It takes me awhile. I want to touch you."

I arch a brow, intrigued by this challenge. "I'm not going anywhere and I'll explode the second you make contact with my cock."

That draws a quiet laugh from her, but she still seems uncertain. "Piper, you're perfect. This is so sexy for me." I kiss the tip of her nose and resume pumping my fingers in and out of her slowly. I pepper kisses along her jaw as she relaxes again, nodding. "Tell me what you like."

"God, Cash, I like all of this." She whimpers as I reach even deeper inside her and I grin when I feel a surge of moisture coat my fingers. I could do this all night, kiss her and fuck her with my hand as she squeezes at her perky tits and wriggles on my couch.

Eventually, something shifts. I feel her start to pulse around my hand and I watch her face as her orgasm approaches. She moans low and deep as I press against her clit and she starts slapping my shoulders before she lets out a shriek. "Fuck, Cash, I'm coming. I'm sorry, I can't be quiet. Oh goooooddddddddd."

I should put a palm over her mouth. I should do a lot of things. But I don't. I just hover above her, continuing to stroke and press as she comes explosively, in a gush of heat, her body thrashing. I let the sight and smell and sound of it sink in, knowing I'll be fantasizing about this moment for months.

As Piper calms down and my own pulse starts to slow, I hear Ruby thrashing in her bed. Not quite awake but certainly not deeply asleep. And that's when I remember that this can't be anything more than a fantasy. I can't fuck women on my couch while my daughter sleeps. I can't have my daughter come downstairs to find me with my pants undone, a raging boner jutting out above our naked neighbor.

I rock back onto my heels and fasten my jeans, swallowing and trying to keep the panic off my face. I scramble, mentally, thinking of what I could tell Ruby if she actually does come downstairs. I have to have an exit plan for any type of sex. Piper doesn't have to worry about that kind of thing. And why should she have to? She *says* she wants family but she doesn't know what family entails.

Piper drapes an arm over her forehead, her chest heaving even as her skin breaks out in goosebumps. "Hey," I whisper. She opens one eye and smiles at me, looking so completely satisfied until she realizes I put my shirt on and zippered up.

She sits up abruptly, looks around for something to cover herself with.

"Piper, that was so sexy. So fucking hot."

She swallows, looking hurt. "I mean, I thought we were just starting..."

I reach past her and pick up her bra with a hooked finger, handing it to her. "I...can't, Piper. I can't."

Time stands still as she stares at me. I don't think either of us breathes until she says, "Right. Ruby."

She stands up and yanks on her leggings. She bends over to get her shirt, her ass an inch from my face, and I know I'm not currently welcomed to touch it. When she faces me again, fully clothed, she's also put on a hard shell, distance. I shouldn't have let things get this far. "Piper..."

"Well I have classes all day tomorrow. Please text me the next time you're ready to record."

She starts to walk toward the back door. "Piper. Don't leave like this."

"You've been very generous. Thank you for the..." She looks up as the springs on Ruby's bed squeak again. I should probably buy her a new mattress. Piper sighs and opens the back door. "I'll talk to you later, Cash."

She closes the door behind her, leaving me alone in the kitchen.

28

PIPER

When I get to the gym in the afternoon, I see that Cash patched up the walls like he'd promised. He must have given up some of his day-job time to do it, because I know he wouldn't leave the house while Ruby was asleep.

After I had a bit of a cry about the way things shook out on Cash's couch, I thought more about what it must be like for him as a single dad. He *has* to put Ruby first, because there's nobody else to prioritize her. I get that. But I can't help but feel like Cash is doing to himself what my mom did to her own health...he's putting himself dead last and it's eating him alive. I know when someone is struggling. Cash may not be one of my moms, but I can see a lot of the same signs that he's struggling.

I know he is into me. Lord, the things he said last night while he was making me come...I don't know if any man has ever been so patient and so seemingly turned on by the process of patiently strumming me to orgasm. I just have to figure out how to get him to see that he can still be an amazing dad and also, you know, date me. I groan, realizing that of course Cash can't do something casual like date. I should have been more considerate of his sleeping daughter last night. I'm going to have to figure out what it means for me to be into him. Do I want to be with a family man?

I bite my lip, and phone a friend.

Esther sounds distracted when she answers with a grunt.

"Did you ever date a guy with kids?"

She whistles. "Did you sleep with him?"

"Not all the way...but...did you? Date someone with kids?"

Esther hums, and I guess she's thinking about it. "I mean I'm sure I've slept with someone who has kids. But I don't date."

I sigh. "That tracks."

"You like him." There's no question in her tone. She's stating facts here. "You like the kid, too. What's the issue?"

I groan. "I don't really think there is one. But he does. I mean...he's super sensitive about...doing stuff...where she might hear. Which we can work on, I think. But it's not like I haven't met her. Why's he being weird?"

I hear a clatter in the background. Esther is always working. I remember that she is my investor in addition to my friend and I try to move some equipment so she thinks I am also working.

Finally, she says, "You *do* know his kid. He's got to be careful who he introduces her to. I wish my mom had been even a little careful about introducing me to her revolving door of assholes."

I laugh at the thought of Cash bringing home a series of girlfriends. But I can see her point. "It's all pretty intense I guess."

"Hang in there, Pipes. You're not going anywhere. You work right behind his house."

I smile at her confidence in my business. I've got more

moms than ever, joining me in the park and at various kid-friendly attractions. I love having Ruby with me as a side-kick, and she seems to love demonstrating partner exercises and ways people can be active with their kids to up their cardiovascular health without hulking out like body builders.

I actually do have one client who is interested in body building as a next-year goal, so I've got big plans to work with her once we are allowed back in my gym with all my gear close to hand.

But what's interesting is the way I sort of feel like I have a built-in family with Ruby and Cash. I know that's silly to think about. Especially when Cash is so opposed to letting anyone in, letting anyone share the load with childcare. I mean, the man has never even hired a babysitter.

I help Ruby with her homework and sometimes braid her hair before school. She shows me her drawings and when we're hanging out so Cash can work, we talk about life.

"Thanks, Esther." I nudge another pile of weights. "Hey, I have to go do more work."

"Get it!"

"Talk soon."

THIS EVENING, Cash is finishing up a round of recordings in the garage and asked us not to disturb him even for food, so Ruby and I make pepperoni rolls together. Obviously I use turkey pepperoni and whole wheat dough, which she wrinkles her nose at, but I think it's a pretty nice compromise.

"How much longer do you think they need?" Ruby

crouches on the floor in front of the oven, shining a flashlight inside because the oven light is broken.

I laugh at the irony of the electrician having electrical issues in his home and bend over to peek in the oven. "The dough still looks pretty mushy."

She looks up at me, confused. "How can you tell?"

I shrug. "I'm not sure how to describe it. It just...seems like it'd be jiggly if I shook the pan."

"Can we shake it and see?" I shrug and open the door, grabbing an oven mitt and giving the pan a jolt. Sure enough, the long tube of hot dough wobbles. Ruby seems impressed and I slide the pan back in the oven.

"Do you have your watch? Let's try ten more minutes. We could do something while we wait and take our minds off it..."

Ruby frowns and sits on the floor in the kitchen. "I don't want to take my mind off it. The bakers on the TV shows always watch their ovens."

I sit beside her. "That's true. They do that, huh?"

Ruby leans her head on my shoulder and I think my heart stops for a moment, I'm so overwhelmed by the trust she's showing me. "You know everything."

I run my fingers through her ponytail and shake my head. "I only know a few things. But I learn more every day!"

"No. You know everything. Like the stuff moms know."

My breath catches as I process her words, not sure how what to say next. Cash was pretty clear that mom-talk is off limits with Ruby. But...I'm not frightened of the idea of Ruby thinking of me as mom-like. This isn't anything I ever consciously yearned for, but now that it's happening, I really like it. We sit together quietly, watching the dough crisp up and eventually brown.

After we pull the food from the oven I let Ruby use the

pizza cutter to slice it, making sure we set a chunk aside for Cash, and I use their lone large knife to cut up some carrot sticks for us. "We have to have at least one vegetable," I explain. "Our bodies need the fiber. And the vitamins."

"What's fiber?" Ruby sticks her tongue out as she slices the pepperoni roll into neat pinwheels, but we both jump when we hear a gruff voice behind us.

"You'll find out about fiber when you're old, kid." Cash pulls the back door shut behind him and smiles. "This smells good." My heart flutters at the sight of him, at the memory of that low voice in my ear.

He dots a kiss on Ruby's head and reaches for the hot pan. I smack his hand away. "You'll burn yourself!"

He laughs, and I don't know that I've ever heard him make that sound before. It feels almost as intimate as our time on that couch. Cash holds up his battered hands. "I don't know if I'd even feel it if I did."

I look down at my own calloused palms and shake my head, slicing the final carrot. "Go on and sit down. You're just in time and we'll bring everything in."

And then...we do. I carry plates of food into the dining room with Ruby like I live here, like this is part of my routine. I realize things are moving in a very specific direction, drumming up feelings I just might be ready to process.

This feels very different from dinner parties at Esther or Chloe's house, where everyone laughs and shouts and pours wine for each other. And it definitely feels different from dinner at Samantha's, because she always has everything catered.

After my mom died, food was about cramming something into our mouths between Dad's work shifts and our activities. If he dated anyone, he certainly never brought them home. Never had them eat with us like this. Am I inserting myself where I don't belong?

I'm quiet at the table as Cash talks to Ruby about her day, explains that he got a lot done with Chloe's audio files. There is a peaceful stillness here at this table and I'm really afraid I'm already attached to it.

Ruby pokes her food with a fork, not wanting to pick up the drippy cheese with her fingers. "How come you're telling stories for Chloe but you don't tell stories to me?"

Cash pulls his face back in mock horror. "What are you talking about, kid? I tell you stories every night at bedtime."

"Those don't count. They're in a book." She takes a defiant bite of her roll and closes her eyes to chew apprecia-tively. I smile.

"Ruby, Chloe's stories are in a book, too. I'm reading the book out loud so people can listen in their cars and stuff."

"It'll be like your dad is telling everyone a bedtime story." I smile at Ruby and then my cheeks flush, remem-bering the content of Chloe's books. Does Cash stand out in the garage and read the sexy parts out loud?

He looks down at his food pointedly as Ruby starts to yawn. By the time the three of us finish eating, Ruby's head is bobbing up and down.

"You really wore her out today." Cash reaches for her plate and props it on his as he heads toward the kitchen.

I follow behind with my plate and the serving bowls. "She showed me mulch mountain in the park, which is apparently a thing."

He nods, rinsing the cheese from the plates. "Ah, yes, the city mulches all the leaves and lawn debris people drop off. Our park is sort of a staging ground until they can distribute the mulch to all the parks."

I smile and scratch at my ankle, where I can still feel the

bits of sticks and leaves itching me. "Well, Ruby was queen of the mountain a few thousand times. No wonder she's ready for bed." We both look in the dining room and see she's put her head down on the table. "I'll wash these. You go take her upstairs."

He shakes his head. "You don't have to wash the dishes, Piper. You're doing us a favor just being here."

I snap a dish towel at him before I drape it over my shoulder. "There's hardly any You go on."

He rolls his eyes and lumbers into the dining room, picking Ruby up with a gentle grunt. I turn to see her sweet face bunched against his shoulder, sticking out in stark contrast to his red hair and dark shirt.

I start to scrub the melted cheese from the sheet pan as he carries her up the steps and I'm doing a fine job pretending it's not sexy as fuck...until I hear him singing to her.

Cash's voice is rich and deep, crooning Bob Marley to his daughter. I clutch the edge of the sink, straining to hear more. I can feel every ounce of parental love in his words, but also the sadness behind them. It's too much.

I sigh and return to my scrubbing, reminding myself that this is the same man who threw a temper tantrum rather than ask me to keep it down. I've almost gotten myself back to neutral, almost stopped imagining what he looks like reading the sexy bits of Chloe's book, when I realize the singing has stopped.

And then I sense him behind me in the kitchen. I feel the heat radiating from his body, smell his deodorant as he approaches. "You didn't have to clean up," he repeats, his voice lower now, softer. Sultry.

I fiddle with the dish towel slung over my shoulder, not wanting to turn around. "I couldn't just leave."

"Why not?" His breath tickles my neck. He's right behind me now, an inch away but not quite touching me anywhere. I could lean back and maybe he'd encircle me in his arms. Maybe he'd take another step back and let me fall...

I spin around slowly and meet his eye. I watch his chest rise and fall with his breath, listen to see if I can hear his heart thundering like my own is inside my chest. "I wanted to hear you sing," I confess, pulling the towel from my shoulder and wadding it up in my hands, a prop to prevent me from reaching out to touch him.

He smiles then, just for an instant, but it shifts his whole face. I love his smiles for how rare they are, am always curious what it was I said that drew them out of him. "You heard that, huh?"

I nod my head. "I loved it." I watch his throat move as he swallows. He stands there still, a hair of space separating us.

"Piper," he whispers, and then closes his eyes. He hangs his head and leans forward, one arm on either side of me, gripping the edge of the sink. I'm boxed in, and I love it. It feels dangerous and thrilling, comfortable and sexy as fuck. I drop the towel. He rests his forehead against mine, and says, "I think we better call it a night."

I feel a chill run through me, followed immediately by a heat wave of frustration. Why is he doing this? Why can't we try? "O-Of course." I try to stoop and pick up the towel, but I can't with him standing so close. I flap my hands, indicating that he needs to back up in order for me to move. "Cash?"

I hope he understands that my question is more than just one word...I'm asking him to reconsider, to give me a chance. Christ, I'd settle for him letting me jerk him off just so I can see what his face looks like when he really lets loose.

He swallows again and uses his hands to shove back from the counter, backing up to give me room. He nods.

"Okay, well..." I tuck my hair behind my ears and bite my lip. I'm suddenly aware of how little time we have left in our arrangement, and I have no idea if he actually has any desire to see me once he's done recording. Maybe he just wants me physically. But if that were true, why wouldn't he let me touch him the other day? I steel myself, control my facial features. "I guess I'll see you tomorrow afternoon."

Cash opens his back door and flicks on the porch light. "See you tomorrow, Piper."

I snatch my key ring from the peg by his back door and rush out to my car so I can high tail it home before I burst into tears of frustration.

29

CASH

IT'S BEEN A WEEK SINCE I CHASED PIPER AWAY AND I'VE managed to sneak in recording sessions without calling her. I've been bribing my daughter to be safe and watch television while I record and...it's been working. I feel weird about it, like I should lean in to this opportunity and call Piper, not for babysitting but because I want to see her. Want to spend time with her.

I immerse myself in work instead.

Ruby is rocking out to Kid Bop in the living room, turning the volume gradually louder as I edit sound files on my laptop in the dining room. Even through my headphones, I can hear the quake of terrible music, but I'm not going to bother asking her to turn it down. This is just my final check for transitions and levels. I can finish this while my kid croons.

And I do. In less time than I thought, I've got the final mastered files to send off to Chloe through the cloud. And... the second they're uploaded I can see that she's already downloading them on her end. She must really be sitting around waiting for this material. I can relate.

My phone pings with a notification that she's paid me, too. I stare at the number on the screen and laugh, knowing this is going to wreak havoc on my taxes this quarter. I laugh even harder, because for the first time I won't have to really worry about the financial implications of that.

Suddenly, the music stops in the living room and the silence in the house feels deafening. I slip off my headphones and see my daughter standing at my elbow. "What's up, kiddo?"

"You were laughing. What's funny?"

I laugh again at her question. "Well, I just got paid a lot of money."

She frowns, confused. "Why is that funny? I don't get it."

I shrug. "I guess it's not. But what should we buy with it?"

I'm not sure what I'm expecting her to say, but she immediately nods and says, "A rat. We should go get the rat from the animal shelter and a really big pen for him to live in. We can name him Isaac."

My eyebrows fly up until I'm sure they'll disappear into my hair. There's no way I'm getting a rodent. I'm just not doing that. Rather than argue with her, I try a distraction technique I saw Sarah using at the playground the other day. "What if I took you and Emerald to the trampoline park instead? Would that be fun?"

Her face lights up and she starts jumping up and down. "Yes! Oh, Daddy, yes! I can re-wear the special socks. But you'll need a pair. Do we have enough extra money for the special socks. It's a rule."

I grin and tell her I'll message Emerald's mom to set everything up. I'm feeling pretty pleased with myself, as much for the successful redirect as the paycheck.

Weekends at the suburban trampoline park are just as terrifying as I imagined. The place is swarming with screaming children who all seem like they're about to break a bone or tear a ligament. But shockingly, nobody seems to get injured. After Ruby helps me select a bright pink pair of required grippy socks, she and Emerald give me a flustered tour of the space, pausing to leap into a foam pit and show me how the zip line works.

I watch them bounce around, and I tentatively follow them for a few minutes before I see a familiar braided pony-tail flopping in the air.

Piper seems like she's leading a class, with a group of moms coordinating their bounces while their kids run literal circles around them on the springy surface. "Piper!" Ruby coos and dashes over with Emerald in tow, joining in the crowd of friends from school whose parents are all evidently avid students of Pipe Fitters.

I sit on a carpeted platform in the middle of the ring of trampolines and watch as Piper greets my daughter with a hug and then returns to her work. Her leg muscles are flexed and taut as she models lunges and jumping jacks. I spend a few minutes admiring the perfection of her body, honed carefully through the course of her work. I try not to think about that body responding to my touch in such a different way, rippling beneath me as I got her off.

That was a mistake. I can't let myself wish for those things. *Can I?* Things feel so much more possible when I'm all charged up like this, high on doing work that fills my soul. I bet this is exactly how Piper feels right now, glowing and smiling while she does what she loves.

She had a similar look on her face the other night, making dinner in my kitchen.

I stare at her some more, wondering if maybe she could feel happy doing family stuff, too. Maybe she could handle the heavy plate I'm always lifting. Eventually I feel like a creep just watching women exercise, so I snag Ruby and Emerald on one of their laps and challenge them to a game of dodge ball.

AN HOUR LATER, we're all dripping with sweat and exhausted, buying sports drinks from a vending machine, when I feel someone tap me on the shoulder. I spin around, blue drink raised to my lips, and try not to spit spray when I see a sweaty Piper, her tank top clinging to her as she stands behind Naomi. Piper seems embarrassed.

Naomi waves at the girls and tells me Zack just received some sort of new Mario video game. "Do you think Emerald and Ruby would want to come back to my house and play it?"

The words are barely out of her mouth before the kids are jumping and squealing with a vigor that seems unimaginable to me. I glance at Piper again, who looks away immediately. I guess I need to figure out how to carry on being neighbors with her now that our deal is complete. Now that there is no obligation between us...is there anything?

I want there to be. God help me, I want there to be something between me and Piper.

I swallow another sip of my drink and tell Naomi that sounds like a great idea. "I'll have to check with Ayana, though, to see if Emerald is allowed."

Naomi's eyes dart between me and Piper and she grins.

"I'll text her right now. It would be so nice for you to have some alone time, Cash. Maybe you could grab some food. Piper, weren't you just telling me that you're starving?"

Oh god, now the Pipe Fitters moms are meddling. I should have seen this coming. I doubt Piper told them anything about our interrupted couch session. But they know as well as me how challenging it is to do anything romantic while parenting a young kid. For years I thought I couldn't manage any form of relationship apart from what I have with Ruby. I can barely manage the school calendar. And Piper deserves more than casual couch fucking. I worry about my ability to manage another obligation and failing to live up to it.

But...fresh from an amazing gig, with money in my pocket and a happy kid...today feels like it's got potential. Except that I might have already mucked things up with Piper by turning her down so many times.

"Aha!" Naomi holds her phone up to show me she got a reply from Ayana. "We're all set. I've got spare boosters in my car. I'll see you in a few hours. Like six hours. Or eight."

And before I can gather a protest, she hustles out the sliding doors with Ruby and Emerald in tow.

30

PIPER

I SHOVE MY HANDS IN THE POCKETS OF MY LEGGINGS, awkwardly looking after Naomi as she leaves with the kids. "So, Naomi was my ride..."

I shake my head, frustrated to be so vulnerable with a man who's been pretty clear that he doesn't want...or isn't able...to date me. Cash sighs. 'I guess you'll need a lift back to the city then." I nod and he holds his arm out, gesturing for me to walk ahead of him out of the trampoline park.

We both squint into the midday sunshine and I adjust my bag on one shoulder so I can push my hair out of my eyes. "Nice day!"

"I don't like small talk," he grunts, walking toward his car. He clicks his key fob to unlock it and then opens the back door before shaking his head, laughing. "Sorry. Habit. I guess you don't want to ride in Ruby's booster seat."

"I don't think I'd fit." He glances at my body and I shiver under his gaze. "I really am hungry...can we stop somewhere?"

He nods and we both climb in to the front seats, buckling without touching one another, which is quite a feat because he's large and the car isn't. I laugh, imagining him wedged inside my Fiat. "Where to?" He arches a brow and I consider.

"I think my friend Esther has a food pop-up stand at her bar today. We should go to Bridges and Bitters."

"Bridges and Bitters? Where's that?" He frowns and pulls out his phone, opening the map app.

"It's in Lawrenceville. We're sort of under dressed, but it'll be fine."

He nods and drapes an arm around the back of my seat to back out of the parking spot. God, that's the sexiest possible thing a man can do. I am dying of want by the time he pulls his arm back to the gear shift, the scent of his deodorant and healthy sweat from jumping wafting through the car like a siren smell. If there is such a thing.

"I turned in the last of the files to Chloe," he says, navigating toward the parkway back to the city. "I wanted to thank you for making that connection. I didn't actually thank you, I don't think."

I can't help but smile at his openness. "You're very welcome. Chloe says it's awesome work. I can't wait to hear it."

He flushes until his skin almost matches his orange hair. "It wasn't what I was expecting..."

"Her book? What do you mean?"

He shrugs and merges onto the highway. "I never read a romance before. I just sort of thought they were..."

"What? Fluffy? Vapid? Bodice rippers?"

He snorts. "Patrick ripped a bodice."

I bite my lip. "Oh my gosh, I bet he's a beast in the bedroom. He was such an alpha male in the last book, even as a side character. Anyway, I'm sure it was a consensual ripping."

Cash nods. "It seemed super consensual. Very."

I laugh, remembering the way Chloe wrote her last heroine, who totally owned her sexuality and desire even in an era where women wouldn't have had a ton of access to information about how their bodies work.

Cash slows as the traffic increases closer to the city. "Narrating a romance novel was pretty enlightening. I actually checked out the first two audiobooks from Chloe's series from the library and got myself all caught up in her characters from colonial Pittsburgh."

"You did?" I turn in the seat so I'm facing him. "When did you have time for all that?"

He laughs and shakes his head. "I had them in my headphones all day while I was out on electrical jobs. I kept looking over my shoulder to make sure there were no kids around."

"They're good, right?"

He nods. "So good." We exit the highway and make our way to Lawrenceville. Soon I can see the brightly painted food truck parked in the prime spot outside Esther's bar. I can't help but feel satisfied knowing I could have squeezed my Fiat in the tiny space in front of the truck, before the hydrant.

Cash drives around the block, eventually pulling into a space and tossing that arm behind my seat again to back in. I grab my bag and pull my sweater from it, feeling a little chilly now that I'm not jumping anymore. "Oh, I meant to tell you, your buddy Ben stopped by yesterday afternoon. Gave me the green light to re-open."

Cash turns to me, beaming. "I'm really glad to hear that."

"Are you?" I grin at him and push open the door to Bridges and Bitters, which leads to an immediate squeal from a very tipsy Chloe.

"Oh my GOD there he is!" She clings to her husband's arm, turning him bodily toward the door and pointing. "That's my new voice of Patrick."

Teddy gives Cash a salute and waves at me. "Hey, Pipes."

"Whatcha got there, Ted?" I tip my chin at Chloe, who is twirling and humming and looking very content.

Teddy drapes an arm around his wife, stabilizing her before she wobbles. "Chloe told me she's letting her hair down because her book came together right on time."

"We're gonna hit a list," she croons and clings to Teddy's arm. "And then we're gonna make a beh-beh." I hug both of them, so happy things are going well for them. Chloe drifts over to Cash and envelops him in a sloppy hug, too. "Cashy. Cash-quatch. Mr. Sexy Voice. How did you get here?"

"He's with me, Chlo." I pat her hand. "We're gonna grab some food. Want anything?" Teddy nods his head vigorously and I give him a thumbs up, making my way to the back room with Cash right on my heels.

He stands closer than necessary as we wait in line for the cart of quesadillas and empanadas. I can feel his breath and I keep thinking he's going to reach out and touch me, but he doesn't. He's quiet as I order and then he gets two of everything, shrugging when I turn to face him. "Someone will eat it," he says, and I nod.

We walk back up front and I smile at Esther, who is in her zone with a line three-deep at the bar. Her hands fly as she mixes drinks and pours beer from some of the taps behind her. Not for the first time, I think about how she should hire some extra help. She gets a spare bartender or two on Friday and Saturday nights, but the bar is truly hopping most of the time now.

I'm the last person to offer her business advice, though, so I just try to find a seat or a table with enough standing room for a hulking Sasquatch and me. I spy a small table off to the side and make a beeline. I do want to visit with my friends eventually, but the smell of the food is making my mouth actually water. I catch Teddy's eye and he relieves me of one of the plates, leaving me alone with Cash and our meal.

"So." Cash sits and takes a bite, face lighting with happiness at the flavor combinations. I follow suit and we both take a few minutes to chew. He swallows. "So." I arch a brow at him and take another bite, inviting him to elaborate. "I haven't heard any booming noise from Pipe Fitters. I was surprised to hear you say Ben let you open back up."

I set the empanadas down and wipe off my hands. "I've been trying to keep it down. One of the neighbors told me there are noise ordinances in this neighborhood..."

Cash chuckles. I love the sound of his laughter. And then I get frustrated because any minute now, he'll freak out about enjoying himself and take the laughter away. Shut me out again. "I've missed having an excuse to come yell at you, Piper."

I frown at him and cross my arms over my chest. "You don't have to yell at me to talk to me, you jerk."

His face falls for a minute and he sets his own food back down on the table. He swallows and leans forward. "What would you say to me if I did come to you for conversation?"

I swallow a lump in my chest, not sure I want to assume anything about what he's asking right now. "It would depend on the nature of the conversation. I don't like getting yanked back and forth. I'm not a rope."

He nods. "I shouldn't have tugged you." He stares at me for a long moment and then says, "I don't know how to do this, Piper. You have to know I'm into you."

"How would I know that?"

He rolls his eyes. "I would have thought that night on the couch would make things obvious."

I recoil and frown. "You practically threw me out in the rain the other night." Cash closes his eyes and swallows hard. I flick his hand on the table. "I just can't handle mixed messages. Either you want me or you don't."

He leans forward and looks me in the eye, his gaze piercing and hot. "I want you Piper. Right now."

31

CASH

"MY CAR COULD NAVIGATE THIS TRAFFIC FASTER." PIPER gloats from the passenger seat as I huff my way around a tractor trailer on my way back to the neighborhood.

"I will concede in this specific instance that your car would be faster." I grind my teeth and finally spy an opening, zooming through a yellow light and squeezing her thigh in celebration once we're moving.

"I accept your concession." Piper sets her hand on top of mine and I let my fingers creep higher on her leg. She smiles and I let myself enjoy it, enjoy putting that expression on her face.

I park behind my garage and turn to face her. "You going to show me the final gym? For conversation?"

She pokes me in the chest with her index finger. "Only if you promise not to freak out, shut me out, or run away after we're done talking."

I nod, solemnly. "I promise."

Piper climbs out of the car and fishes around her bag for her keys. "I get checkups all the time, you know. I have a clear bill of health."

She meets my eye over her shoulder before she unlocks the door. The subtle smell of fresh paint and cleaner greets us. I swallow and step inside. "I...uh...haven't slept with anyone in years."

Piper nods. "Okay." She produces a condom from her bag, drops the bag on the floor, and grins. "Allow me to refresh your muscle memory."

I feel my body relax just that much more that Piper isn't weirded out about my lack of recent experience. And then she shoves me in the chest and I fly backward, my ass landing on one of her truck tires. I drop my arms back to catch myself and Piper straddles me, sinking onto my lap as her lips sink onto mine. This feels so different from last time, when I couldn't unwind for fear of waking Ruby. I don't need to be on watch right now.

I wrap her hair around my fist and tug and Piper grins. She likes this side of me. She bites my lip and I pinch her nipple through her shirt and we both laugh as she rips off my shirt. Her skin tastes salty from exertion and it turns me on.

"I want you," I breathe. "I want you all the time."

Piper grabs hold of my chest hairs and tugs, snapping me back to attention. "Take your sweats off," she commands, and I lift my hips from the tire just enough to follow her instructions. I hiss when she grabs my cock in her fist and gives me a firm tug.

"Oh my," she says, studying my junk. "I've never been with anyone uncircumcised."

My breath comes quickly as she jerks me a few times, experimenting with the skin on my shaft. "Well, uh, I guess it all works the same way. Fuck!" She dips her head and licks my tip, exploring. Piper pulls her leg back behind her, twisting until she's on her knees on the floor mats in between my legs, scrutinizing my dick like it's a puzzle she's trying to solve.

"This part just rolls up and down, huh?" She experiments and it feels great.

I nod and swallow, gripping the tire for balance when she lowers her mouth back over the tip. "Mmm," she says, popping off the end. "I see how it works."

"Get back up here," I growl, hauling her back onto my lap as she strips out of her leggings. Once again, she's not wearing panties and as she settles on my lap, I feel the slick heat of her rocking against me. Both of us moan as she tilts her hips.

She keeps rocking her wetness on my cock as I peel her tank top and bra off and she moans my name when I drop my mouth to her nipple, mimicking the motion she used with her tongue on my tip. Both of us are frantic, squirming and squeezing, kissing and moaning until she climbs off my lap again, pouncing toward her clothes and rummaging for the condom. "I can't take it anymore," she pants. "I need you inside me."

I'm not going to argue with her. Not when she rips open the condom and rolls it slowly over my length. Not when she grins and climbs back onto my lap, lining me up and then sinking onto me as she supports her weight on my shoulders. Every cell of my body is alight with sensation as she takes me into her body.

I'm afraid to close my eyes, to look away from the goddess now bouncing on my lap, using the spring of the tire to help with the rhythm.

"Fuck, Piper. Fuuuckkk." She nods, planting her feet on the mats and using those rock-hard thighs of hers to slam up and down, riding me hard like only a fitness instructor could manage. I'm here for the show, staring at her breasts bouncing, searing the expression on her face into my memory.

"Yes, Cash, god, that feels good." She adjusts her angle, tilting forward so those nipples drag up and down my chest as she moves. "I love being close to you like this." I'm not going to last much longer, especially knowing she's as into this as I am. I pull one hand from the tire and reach in between us, finding that bundle of nerves she guided me to last time. I look into her eyes as I circle her clit and Piper slows her bounce, moaning loudly.

Soon, we are moving together in slight rocking thrusts. Together, we are creating this forcefield of pleasure, this shimmering halo of everything I've ever wanted. "Harder," she whispers, and pulls a hand from my shoulder to press my thumb tighter against her body. "I need it so hard, Cash." I nod, extremely turned on by her telling me just what she needs to get off, even more turned on that I get to be the one to give it to her.

I feel the pulses starting inside her, rings of throbbing muscle around my cock and I watch in awe as she comes with my name on her lips. I start to believe this is possible for me, not just today but every day. I can share things with her, tell her what I need and trust her to give it to me like she's trusting me to give her what she needs in this moment.

"Cash, I'm coming so hard!" She screams and bites my ear lobe and shudders in my lap and I burst into flames, grunting as my hips thrust up and I spill into the condom again and again, her name on my lips, my voice hoarse from shouting my own release.

When the waves pass, I don't want to run. I don't panic. I pull her tighter against me, like she's anchoring me to the earth, and I let her hold me in return. We did this together. As a team. I feel this shimmer of hope zap between us, like maybe it's possible we could work. Long-term. Maybe this electric woman could be mine, along with Ruby and work. I hold her until my legs grow numb and my lower back threatens to spasm.

Eventually she rolls backward off my lap, plopping onto the floor like a snow angel, limbs splayed, looking blissfully fucked. "That was amazing,' she says, her voice low and languid.

I crawl on my belly to join her and pepper her shoulders with kisses until I hear my phone vibrating persistently.

Grudgingly, I pull it close to me, squinting to see the messages on the screen. It's a series of texts from Ayana.

"What's up," Piper asks, eyes closed and limbs leaden.

I drop a kiss on her forehead and smack her flank. "Ayana is getting Ruby and Emerald and keeping them overnight. Let's get you into my bed."

32

PIPER

I WAKE UP PRESSED INTO THE MATTRESS BY THE BULKY BODY OF Cash Brennan, and I love it. After he dragged me into his house caveman-style, we got to experience making out on an actual bed, with plenty of room to move around. And it was glorious.

I smile, remembering the ninja twists I executed and the way he knelt behind me, pressing my shoulders into the mattress while he thrust into me with savage strength.

I only had a three-pack of condoms, so we still have a lot of maneuvers to practice once one of us gets to the pharmacy. I wriggle out from beneath Cash and head downstairs to make coffee, leaning against the wall and thinking about what a turn my life has taken.

Am I really diving into this relationship? There is so much about Cash that makes sense. He's thoughtful, even if he'd never admit it. And he's so passionate. As an athlete myself I've always been drawn to goal-driven people. I think back on Cash's expression as he talked about his work for Chloe, as he told me about finishing the project.

And now he's naked and I'm drenched in the laundry

smell of his sheets and his skin. I smile. It's been a tumultuous autumn, speeding between a rushed opening, an abrupt closure, and now an intentional grand celebration to honor the mission and clients of Pipe Fitters.

I hear a grumble and a thump from upstairs and realize Cash has awoken. I decide to pour him a coffee and set to work searching his fridge for milk. I usually put skim in mine but he's only got whole milk, presumably for Ruby.

I hear him stomp into the kitchen and my entire body threatens to melt with joy when he slides up behind me to kiss my neck as I stare into his fridge. "You probably drink it black," I say, leaning my head against his as he continues to nibble my neck.

"Like my soul." He plants a final kiss near my ear and grabs the steaming mug from the counter.

I accept that my choices are whole milk or nothing, and I do not have a black soul, so I splash in some of the milk. I lean against the counter, sipping and smiling at Cash, who sips and smiles back. "I like this," I tell him. The corner of his mouth hooks up in a grin, his face content like it was last night after our third condom.

It feels thrilling and secret to see him this way. Dare I say he's relaxed?

He opens his mouth to say something to me but then his phone starts chirping. "Ah," he says, sliding it out of his sweatpants pocket. "That's my alarm to go get Ruby."

"Oh."

I can't hide my disappointment that our blissful escape is ending. Of course he has to get his daughter, and of course we have to be really careful with what she sees. I already know I'm attached to her, and I'm an adult with mature feelings. We have a lot to discuss. Cash pushes off the counter and crosses over to wrap his arms around me.

It's such a caring gesture, another glimpse of surprising depth I'm just beginning to savor. I lean my cheek against his shoulder, celebrating the hug. This is every bit as nice as the hugs from my students. Maybe even a little nicer, since I know this one is a rarity—that I've drawn this tenderness out of this grizzly bear of a man. He murmurs into my hair, "I can't wait to see you again. But I have to keep this separate for now."

I nod my head. I understand that. And I know he's not ashamed of me, not keeping me secret. Every one of my friends saw his hands all over me as we fled Bridges and Bitters yesterday en route to our sex-capades in the gym.

I can't quite pinpoint why this crashing arrival of reality feels like a derailed train after the evening we just shared.

I unwrap myself from Cash's arms and set my mug in the sink. "I gotta locate all my stuff..." I look around the house at the trail of socks and sports bras and random garments we threw off each other as we fumbled in his back door and through the house to the staircase.

Cash and I pick it all up together, quietly sorting his things from mine. "Last night was incredible," he says, dangling one of my shoes toward me with one of his small, crooked smiles. "Piper, I...I've been treading water for a long time. I'm trying to let people toss me a rope."

"Back to the rope metaphors..."

"Come one. Cut me some slack." He winks and mimes tugging on a rope. "I'd like to try. I like you. I like that you drive me bananas. I like that you're perpetually cheerful. I like that you're nice to my kid."

"Your kid is amazing."

He nods. "You're amazing, though. Everything about you." I blink at him, not sure what to say. He rests a hand on mine and swallows. "I want to try, Piper. But I'm rusty. I can only try things slowly."

I relax my shoulders. "I'm okay with slow." Except...I can feel his eagerness for me to skedaddle so he can go pick up his daughter.

Maybe I feel nervous because the next time I see Ruby, I'm going to see Cash, too, and I'm not going to be able to slide my hands in his pants pockets or pinch his nipples. I'm going to have to hold back just when I finally got him to let loose.

He must sense what I'm thinking, because he leans close and whispers into my ear. "I have to figure out how to tell Ruby about us, okay?" He leans back and meets my eye. I swallow. "She's never had someone around...I want to do this right."

I nod rapidly. He's right. I know this. It still feels big. I know I'm not being dismissed, but maybe I didn't take time to consider the full weight of entering into this with him. He kisses my knuckles. "I feel like there are other things I haven't done right, Piper. And it's important to me that this." He gestures between us. "This feels right and I want to address it the right way with Ruby."

"There's no rush," I mutter, as much to myself as to Cash.

He nods and hands me my sweatshirt. "We should celebrate this week, though. Your gym...my book. The empanadas didn't count."

A spark of warmth simmers in my belly at his words. "You mean like a date?"

He nods. "Yeah, Piper. Can I take you on a date?"

I poke his shoulder. "I'll have to consult my schedule."

"You do that." He grins as I slip out the front door.

33

CASH

I HAVE NO IDEA WHERE TO TAKE A WOMAN LIKE PIPER ON A date. She doesn't seem like a dinner and a movie kind of gal...plus I haven't been to a movie since high school.

But the bigger problem is what to do with Ruby Wednesday night when Piper and I both realized we were free in the evening. My parents have banjo night and despite my pleading with them to take Ruby along for the music, they put their foot down about it.

This leaves me in the very uncomfortable position of having to speak to the other parents at the school bus stop Tuesday afternoon as we wait for our kids to arrive. I shake my shoulders to get loose and find myself doing some of my voice exercises, wiggling my jaw and breathing deeply, until I realize that must make me look like some sort of weirdo.

Finally, I groan and just approach the least-flustered looking mom at the corner. "Hey, can I ask you something?"

She looks up from her phone, startled. Her pale cheeks are pink in the crisp air and the knot of hair on top of her head blows around in the wind as she tries to decide if I'm terrifying. I attempt a smile and she shrugs.

"Do you have a babysitter you can recommend?"

Her mouth drops open for a moment and she tilts her head in confusion. Another mom pops her head up from her phone and leans in to see what we're talking about. The first mom nudges the other, a woman I recognize from our block but have never spoken to before. The first one says, "We all just swap kids if we need to go out. We all figured you were some kind of hermit or something."

The second woman nods.

"Hmm." I shove my hands in my pockets and squint toward Penn Avenue, wishing the bus would either show up or a sink hole would swallow me and spare me the embarrassment of having to explain myself. "Well, I kind of am a hermit. But I'm working on it." I pause for a second as they blink at me. "I'm Cash. My kid is Ruby. She's in second grade."

"I'm Toi," says the second mom. "And we know Ruby. She's a year ahead of my Bryson." The women exchange glances and a third mom jogs to the corner, looking relieved to see us all still here. I don't know why I never talked more to the other parents on my street. Maybe because I was a teenager when I became a parent and I was too busy drowning to look around for any kind of life preserver.

The late mom, a fellow redhead with a low bun and professional office attire, sags against the street sign. "What did I miss? I got stuck in traffic."

"You're fine," Toi assures her. "Bus isn't even here yet." She points at me. "Cash here has finally decided it's safe to talk to us. He needs a sitter."

Office mom perks up. "Oh. You're Ruby's dad, right? She's a year younger than my twins. When do you need help? I'm not going anywhere this week. Soccer just ended."

Could it really be this easy? Maybe easy is the wrong

word. I see how these parents are all looking out for each other, and I know it involves a lot of give as well as a lot of take. I haven't felt capable of giving anything in a long time.

But then I remember what I just achieved. I found a way to fix Piper's wiring and work on a narration project, and Ruby was fine. I'm fine. I can do this. I swallow. "I, um, have a date? Tomorrow evening."

Toi smiles widely. "A date! That's exciting. Definitely send Ruby to Margo's house. Margo won't even notice she's in there and Ruby will come home with her nails painted galaxy glitter."

Office mom, Margo, rolls her eyes. "I threw away the nail polish, I swear. Cash, please feel free to send Ruby down. How late will you be? My kids start bedtime around 9."

The bus rumbles up and the kids pile off, screaming and laughing. Ruby pulls ahead of them like always, running toward me. But this time I realize that she's stopping her conversations with the neighbor kids in order to pull to the side where I usually stand, alone.

Maybe I assumed my kid was an island in the storm, like me, but Ruby's got friends. Ruby isn't the one struggling here. I guess I should feel thankful for that. "Thank you, Margo." I put a hand on Ruby's shoulders as Margo's twins dig around Margo's purse for the house keys. "I'd love to take you up on that."

MARGO and I exchange numbers and settle on logistics, and she has a great suggestion for my date with Piper: axe throwing. I feel deeply satisfied with this choice when Piper squeals in delight over the phone. "We have to wear flannel," she says. "And think of lumberjack names to use. Also I'm going to kick your ass."

"I'm sure you will," I tell her.

I walk Ruby over to Margo and the twins' house around five on Wednesday and wave to the dude I assume is Margo's husband. He doesn't really look up from his laptop, which is fine because I don't have time to make small talk. I want to use every minute of this window to spend time with Piper, so I kiss the top of Ruby's head and smile as she disappears into our neighbor's house.

Piper is waiting outside her building as I pull up, wearing tight jeans and a flannel knotted at her waist. Shit, she looks good. I can see her belly button peek out beneath the ends of the flannel and I can't wait to stand behind her and trace that little divot.

She squeezes my hand as we walk through the gravel lot to the axe throwing joint. "I decided this is a little like being vikings, so my lumberjack name is more of a shield maiden name." She bites her lip and bounces on her feet as we wait in line to pay. "I'm going to be Hilda," she whispers into my ear, and I'm not focused on her words so much as the feel of her breasts against my arm. "It means fighter. What's your name?"

"Yours," I tell her. "I'm yours."

She flushes and then swats my arm. "Okay, that's really sweet. But seriously, Cash, you need a name or I'm not play-ing. And I know you want me to play."

I do want to play with her. I want to let loose with her and challenge her. But I have no fucking idea what fake name to use while axe throwing. "Isn't Cashel exotic enough?"

She taps her chin and pulls out her phone as we step

closer to the desk to check in. "What about Angus? It's Gaelic for strength."

"Angus and Hilda? Those are our date names?" She nods and I sigh, signing us in for a lane and filling in our chosen names on the forms.

We wait impatiently for our instructor to show us the ropes, and I make good and sure the instructor and Piper both know I'm with her throughout our lesson. It feels nice to be affectionate in public, to drape my arm around her waist and let my fingers explore that naval I know I want to lick the next time we're alone together.

After Piper sinks a few bullseyes in a row hurling the axes one handed, the instructor nods, impressed, and decides we're ready to be alone in the lane. Good.

I lean on the wooden rail just watching as Piper grips an axe in each hand and looks back over her shoulder, then winks at me before growling just like a viking shield maiden and whipping each axe at the target. "Ha! Hilda!" She jumps in the air, having sunk a bullseye and a three-point shot. This was apparently an amazing date suggestion, because she's having a terrific time out there.

"You're up, Angus." Piper slaps my ass and grins as she sets the axes on the safety stump. I take a stance like the instructor recommended, throwing the axes one at a time with two hands on the handle. I hit the target, which feels like a victory. I enjoy the satisfying thwack sound as the axe sinks into the wood. I feel like a kid—joyful, playful. I can't believe I'm getting to experience this after so many years of just clenching everything.

I take a step back to line up my second shot and glance over my shoulder to see Piper leaning on the rail, rapt, studying me just as carefully as I did her. I take a breath to steady myself, overcome by the sensation of being near someone so interested in me, so interesting to me.

I throw the axe and miss the target, but I don't care. I saunter back to kiss my girl, right there in public, like I've been doing it my whole life. She keeps it brief, though, pulling back and putting her hands on my shoulders. "You gotta go retrieve the axes, Angus, so I can take my turn. That's how this works."

I nod my head. "I see. You're more interested in winning than kissing."

Piper laughs and shakes her head. "Cash. You can't take me to an athletic competition site without activating my intense need to dominate."

I sigh and walk up to the target and pull out the axe, stooping to pick the other up from the ground and then sticking them both in the safety stump. "This seems sort of antithetical to the mission of Pipe Fitters. What happened to just increasing movement and general health?"

Piper hip checks me out of the way and pulls the axes from the stump, adjusting her grips on the handles. "That's work, Angus. This is play. And I play to win." As soon as I back up over the blue line on the floor, Piper grunts and hurls the axe. Another bullseye. I'm more than a little turned on. When she throws the second axe, I tell her I'm going to the bar to get us some drinks, that she should go ahead and take my turn for me.

She shrugs, and sets herself up to do just that.

As I'm walking back to our axe lane with our beers, I see Ben walking in with a group of guys in polo shirts and badges. These must be his inspector buddies. "Ben," I say, tilting my chin at him.

"Cash!" He seems startled to see me, which makes sense because I rarely leave my house in the evening. "Shit, man, what are you doing here?"

I grin and gesture toward my lane. "I'm on a date."

Ben grins and grips my upper arm. "Hey, good for you, man." He follows my gaze to the lane, where Piper sinks another one-handed bullseye and pumps her fist, grunting about Hilda. I can't help but smile at her, because she's cute as hell. "Oh," Ben says, and then he whistles.

"What?" I turn toward him, frowning.

He groans and stuffs his hands in his pockets. "Eeeee, she's really not going to like talking to me. I have bad news for her."

"What sort of news? She said you gave her the green light to open."

Ben scratches his head and waves a hand at his colleagues, who are approaching the check-in table. "Yeah, she's good to go. For now. The thing is the building owner just sold to developers. The whole place is going to be shut down. Condos." He shakes his head and exhales through his nose.

I feel my stomach clench, a ball of acid hanging out in the back of my throat. "Doesn't she have any recourse? That's really fucked up, man."

Ben holds his palms up. "I'm just the inspector. I'll be out there next week to make sure it's okay to sell, for the developer to move forward with the construction. Sorry, man. Hey, do me a favor and wait to tell her until she puts the axe down?"

I take a long pull of my beer, staring at Piper, who bends to pull the axes from the stump again and hurls them at the target, one-two, like I was afraid she'd do with the sledge hammer that day in the alley. The thought of being the one to tell her this news makes me feel nauseated. How the hell does this happen on the one, single date night I've had this decade? I just really, really wanted a night to be out with her. Ben reminds me how fleeting nice things are. If tonight is all I get, I'm not tarnishing it. "I'm not telling her a damn thing," I tell Ben. "That's your job. I'm not going to be the one to crush her. I just got her to tolerate me."

Ben shrugs and backs toward the check-in. "Your choice. Thanks, I guess? See you."

I make my way back to Piper, who lights up at the sight of me. "Angus," she says, nodding her head toward the axe. "I do believe it's your turn."

I kiss the tip of her nose and hand her a beer. I'll be damned if I ruin this date, and fuck Ben for telling me that information in the first place. I take one more sip of my beer and approach the stump, not caring that I'm losing the game as long as I'm here with Piper.

34

PIPER

"Of course you won at axe throwing," Samantha says. "It was never going to be a contest. I will concede that Cash-quatch chose an acceptable date for you, Piper. He knows you well. I approve."

I grin, and not just because the decals on the wall look fantastic. I ordered those inspirational quotes I wanted, but in sticker form, so I can peel them off periodically and change them out. Despite my insistence that I didn't need any help, my friends drove over after work to help me put the finishing touches on Pipe Fitters ahead of my grand opening this weekend.

"Samantha, this is way too much food. It's a *gym.*" I know my protests are futile as Samantha unloads cases of snack bags of raw almonds and oranges. Samantha Vine always buys too many gifts for Foof friends. We love her despite the excess.

"I can't hear you over the crinkling of these bags," Sam says, hefting another case of almonds onto the folding table she also bought me. "Don't worry. These were ethically sourced and processed with recycled water." She nods solemnly enough that I make a mental note to go look up almond processing and see what that's all about.

Chloe and Esther march around with a sketch, pointing out where I'll set up the vendor tables on Saturday. I've got Judy the bra whisperer coming to sell sports bras and offer fittings. She says she has a portable dressing room she can bring for privacy so I just need to leave her some space that I mark off with a pile of tires, blushing a little at the memory of my last time using those rubber rings.

Esther squints at the sketch and raises a dark brow at me. "What the hell is pelvic floor therapy?"

I smile. "It's exercises and things to repair the pelvic floor after childbirth."

She frowns. "Do I even want to ask?"

I shrug. "Things get a little messed up down there, to put it mildly. But there are techniques to help! Most of my clients pee when they jump rope, but that doesn't need to be the case." I tape a sign to the wall beneath the pull-up bars, where I plan to set up the physical therapist.

I think I'd be bouncing around even if the floor mats hadn't arrive to give the entire place a springy step. "I'm just so excited, guys."

"And we are excited for you," Sam says. "As I said, I'm going to come do an exercise with you on Saturday. So you know that means I'm hyped."

"Just one exercise?" Every now and then I can get the gals to go on walks with me, but apart from Chloe, the Foof ladies aren't too into the gym life. I tease them a little more about avoiding my services, but Esther reminds me how many kegs and cases of alcohol she hauls around every day of the week. She flashes me her bicep for emphasis and I give it a squeeze, appreciatively. "You're right. I am always emphasizing the importance of incorporating movement into every day life. Thank you, Esther."

"Yeah, yeah. You can still tease me, you know that, Piper? Giving shit to each other is a sign of respect."

Esther grew up with a lot more siblings than I did, so I take her word for it and nod. And then I twirl around in a circle from pure happiness that Pipe Fitters is finally taking shape. I'm finally opening my doors to a full slate of clients committed to emphasizing their health. I could clap my hands...except I see Ben the city inspector standing in my doorway along with Alessio, the building owner.

Ben winces when he sees Esther, but waves timidly with the hand not holding a clipboard. "Hey, ladies. Wish I were here under different circumstances."

Esther crosses her arms over her chest. "What's that supposed to mean? Piper jumped through every hoop you laid out for her. Just look at this place."

Ben smiles and pats the newly-painted white walls. "It does look great. Truly. Unfortunately, Alessio here has decided to sell the property to a development company."

Alessio grins, giving me a smarmy smile. "Love what you've done with the place. Timing was just off, sweetheart."

Samantha is in his face in a flash, index finger pointing at his yucky chest. "Don't you call her that. Don't you dare use that term."

He holds his hands up mockingly. "Easy now. I made a business decision. The developer will take over the lease, but I'm fairly certain they'll be buying you out." He shrugs.

"This is breach of contract." Samantha is practically snorting with rage and I'm almost sure I can see steam coming out of her ears. Or maybe that's steam from the fire spewing out of Esther's eyes. Either way, I feel super supported as I try to make sense of what is happening here.

Ben clears his throat. "The most likely scenario in these instances is that you'll be offered a break in the lease."

Sam taps her high-heeled toe. "What about the money she invested into this physical space? The electrical replacement?" Ben scratches at his chin, looking uncomfortable. Sam flares her nostrils at Alessio. "You'll be hearing from Ms. Conklin's attorney." I don't bother telling Samantha I don't have one. I suspect she'll be lending me one of hers from Vinea or else strong-arming someone from Foof into checking over all this paperwork.

"I'm really sorry about this, Piper. The place looks great." Ben hands me a form letter from the city with bullet points and typos. I can barely make out the letters as tears well up in my eyes.

All this work, all this investment into a space that any normal person would never have rented to begin with. I knew it was too good to be true, this idea that I could create some sort of oasis. That it could be me at the helm.

As Ben and Alessio walk out, leaving the door open behind them, my friends crush me in a hug. Even Esther pats my shoulder, and she normally eschews physical contact. "We're going to figure this out, Pipes," she whispers. "You've got a good thing going here."

I stifle down a scream and march over to the wall where I hung my grand opening banner, complete with iron pipe graphics. I rip the sign down and tear it in half, growling, before I sink to the floor in tears.

35

CASH

Once again, I hear a knock at my back door. I've grown fairly certain it's Piper whenever that happens, so I don't think twice before striding through the kitchen to open up. Ruby's just gone up to bed, so I also don't want the knocking to continue any longer than necessary.

"Hey," I say as I pull the door open, but then I freeze, because Piper is sobbing. "Hey," I repeat, my voice softer now as I tug her hand and pull her into the kitchen. I wrap her in a hug, taking a brief moment to feel pride at this instinct. Maybe I do know how to be in a relationship...

But I quickly realize why Piper is probably sobbing, and I'm not sure how to proceed.

"Cash," she snorts, her breath coming in hiccups. "It's all falling apart."

"I know," I tell her, smoothing a hand down her hair.

"I worked so hard. And they're shutting me down all over again and this time there's not anything I can even do about it."

"I know," I repeat, trying to sooth her with hugs and

empathy, like I've shown my daughter. Like Piper has shown both of us.

Piper cries softly against my shoulder and then stiffens. "Wait. How do you know?" She draws her head back and looks at me in confusion. I purse my lips.

I don't want to lie to her. I'm no expert but even I know that would be a bad move. "I, uh, ran into Ben."

She nods but steps back from me. "And...you didn't come over to the gym? Or call me?" She gestures wildly. "I could have used some support, Cash. Ben was so distant today breaking the news, like I was just some checkmark item or something. What did he say to you this afternoon?"

I blow out a breath. I know I could lie and pretend he swung through my house on the way out of the gym today. But I can't build anything with Piper on a foundation of faulty wires. I scratch at the back of my neck. "Cash?" Piper crosses her arms over her chest protectively, squeezing herself.

"So, I saw him on Wednesday. At the axe place. He told me then." Her eyes widen in disbelief and I nod. "I should have said something to you, Piper. I know that. But..." I pound a fist on the stove top.

"You let me spend days planning my grand opening. I booked vendors, Cash. I paid them for their time for Saturday. You...I could have spent that time looking for another space. What is wrong with you?"

I tug at my hair. "I wanted you, okay? I wanted to continue having a good fucking night with a woman I like and not lose a second of that date to heavy shit. I wanted one god damned day where I could enjoy myself as an adult, out with another adult."

Piper flings her arms wide. "What about Thursday then?

What the fuck? How could you be so inconsiderate and self-centered?"

Piper's voice reaches a pretty impressive volume and I'm not surprised when Ruby pads into the kitchen in the middle of it. "Why is there yelling?"

But I don't look at my daughter. I glare at Piper and snarl, "Since when am I self-centered? I never get to do things for myself. My entire life revolves around caring for my daughter. You are the one fucking thing I've done for myself in seven years, so yeah. I kept that information to myself to preserve another few days of happiness where I could pretend you could actually be my girlfriend!"

Ruby claps her hands. "You said so many red words, Cash."

"Not now, Ruby."

Piper digs her palms into the wall behind her, like she's a second away from using her arms to launch herself at my throat.

Ruby tugs at my shirt. "Are you and Piper going to get married? Isn't that what girlfriends and boyfriends do?"

Piper breathes through her nose like a trapped animal. "No, Ruby, sweetie. We aren't getting married. Your dad was fooling around when he said 'girlfriend.'" She clenches her jaw and speaks through her teeth, looking only at Ruby. "I have to leave. I'll see you at Ayana's house sometime soon, though, okay?"

She flings open the back door before I can refute her argument. With a final glance over her shoulder, Piper snarls, "Consider our *relationship* shut down, too."

36

PIPER

There's no way I can tolerate the crowd at Bridges and Bitters on a Friday night, even if Esther would give the best advice out of all my friends.

I send an S.O.S. into the Foof group chat, hoping that at least someone will be available since my friends aren't really the type to go out clubbing every week.

FOOF CHAT

Things are worse now, guys. Is anyone home?

SAM:

What could be worse? Who should I dox?

CHLOE:

Sam, honey, please don't dox anyone. There are other forms of revenge. And Piper, I'm home. Do you want to come chill in the cottage and we can talk in privacy?

SAM:

I'm coming over. I'll bring Juniper and her lawyer brain.

JUNIPER STAG:

Guys, I've got four kids and it's almost
Halloween. I really can't tonight.

SAM:

Oh my god, I will buy your kids costumes
and have candy delivered to your house.
Junie, we need you.

EMMA STAG:

June, Ty has the kids all being Waldo this
year. We picked up the striped shirts and
hats today! You're good.

JUNIPER:

Well, shit. Who are we going to sue?

> This isn't even about the business stuff.
> Although maybe I should sue my landlord?

LOGAN BRADY:

Piper, we just finished a great product
launch at Vinea so I have lots of capacity to
advise you on business stuff. I'm putting on
shoes to head to Chloe's. What's up
right now?

> Cash-quatch. Things are fucked.

ESTHER:

Hey, guys, it's wild here tonight. What did
Cash-quatch do? Things looked pretty cozy
just a few days ago…Hilda and Angus and
whatnot…

SAM:

I'll fill you in after. Or call you for bail. One of
those. See you soon, Pipes.

I wipe my nose with my arm, not even caring that that's
gross, and drive to Chloe's house in Highland Park. I love
that she and Teddy bought a house with an on-site cottage.

By day, that's where Chloe runs her publishing empire. Right now, she greets me at the door with a glass of wine and a fuzzy-sweatered hug. Not in that order, because obviously Chloe isn't going to spill the wine.

I sink into her couch and sigh when her dog T.K. jumps onto my lap. He licks at my tears, which shocks me enough that I laugh.

"You're such a weirdo, T.K." Chloe snaps her fingers and he sinks down into my lap, resting his head on my knee. I pet him and sip at the wine as Samantha and Juniper burst through the front door with Logan right behind.

"I had to park on the street," Logan huffs. "And I have Cal's Bronco, so..."

Sam winces. "I'm surprised it hasn't been sideswiped yet. That thing is so obnoxiously big." Logan shrugs and they all wedge onto the couch with me. "Okay, Pipes. Spill."

AN HOUR LATER, we've drunk a lot of wine and the Foof ladies seem to have found some more fucks. And they're directing allllll those fucks at cursing Cash Brennan.

"I mean, you hired a vagina therapist." Emma Stag rolled in late but was quickly caught up on the details. She shakes her head and pats my knee from where she's curled on the carpet, petting T.K. "Like, I get that he wanted to pretend things were terrific with you guys, but what did he think would happen?"

I huff. "I don't think he thinks about the future. Or, I don't know, he *only* thinks about the future. Or something." I clutch at my chest. "I can't believe I let him in after how things started off with us."

On one side of the room, Juniper has logged in to

Chloe's computer and is searching landlord and tenant law and cases from some legal databases. Sam is frantically texting the group chat to keep Esther and the others in the loop and all of our phones keep vibrating and chirping. It feels a little like I'm back in the massage chair at the nail salon.

Chloe looks over her shoulder. "I feel like I need to be really clear that I'm going to continue working with him, professionally." She winces. "Good narrators don't just grow on trees and, frankly, I need that sexy baritone to help me sell my books."

"Good," Sam yells. "Objectify him! Earn money off his sweat. Can you at least pay him less or something?"

We all throw pillows at Sam, careful not to spill any remaining wine. "Some of us care about business owners," I mutter. "Some of us set aside interpersonal strife in the best interest of courtesy when it comes to business."

Logan pats my arm. "You're a good person, Piper. That's why your clients love you. While Juniper figures out who to sue and for what, can I distract you from heartbreak by showing you some real estate listings?"

She has her laptop propped open and bites her lip. I let my head sink to the back of the couch, feeling a little woozy on top of my hurt and confusion. "Sure," I murmur. "I'm sure there are loads of places in my price range, zoned for commercial use, located in the East End where most of my clientele lives..."

"That's the spirit." I hear Esther's voice come through my pocket, a little tinny and muffled by fabric and background noise. I must have pocket dialed her. I laugh and wave at Logan to show me what she's found.

Unsurprisingly, she has not found anything that meets my parameters for the business.

I let my eyes close, surrounded by my friends and woozy from the wine.

THE NEXT TIME I open my eyes, I'm alone in Chloe's bungalow, wrapped in a fuzzy blanket, with aspirin and a glass of water on the table near my head.

Alone for the first time since I found out my business is destroyed, I feel deafened by the quiet of the room and my pounding thoughts. I know, rationally, that Esther isn't going to bug me about the loan. That doesn't stop me from feeling like a huge failure about it.

Is bankruptcy a thing? Would I be able to pay Esther back if I declared that? I don't have the energy to call Logan and ask her right now.

How could Cash let me wander into that blind? I thought he cared about me. I told him things about me, private things. I didn't just have sex with him. I opened up to him, to his family. And now it's costing me my mother's legacy.

37

CASH

I can't drum up the energy to talk to Ruby about what happened. She's standing in our back yard, staring across the alley at Pipe Fitters as if someone will come and rip down the CLOSED INDEFINITELY sign and replace all the flags and banners that were intended for the grand opening.

Ruby asked a lot of questions, cried a lot, and danced on the couch for a long time. I wish I had that capacity to let my feelings out loud like that. I know I messed up. I was always going to mess this up.

I never imagined things would be permanently easy...I just thought I'd get more than a week of a relationship this time before it all went to shit.

I could blame Ben for laying that on me. I could blame Alessio for being a shitty landlord and renting to Piper when he knew damn well he was going to sell. But I'm not doing those things. I'm moping around my house in a stained undershirt and old shorts.

At least I'm trying to mope. I'm interrupted by a tap on the front door. This is a new one. It's probably a salesman or someone with religious pamphlets. I try to sink lower on the couch but whoever it is leans to the left and taps on my front window.

It's Margo. I groan and walk to the door, grunting in greeting.

"Hey, Cash, sorry, but Kevin got called in to work this morning and the twins are in rare form. Could they hang out over here while I run errands?" She peers past me at the living room, where Ruby threw a bunch of stuff all over the place and I haven't bothered to pick it up or yell at her to do so. I shrug.

"I don't really know what to do with kids who aren't mine..."

Margo waves a hand. "Oh, just ignore them unless there's blood. Thanks a million, Cash. Do you need milk or eggs? You probably will by the time the girls leave. I'll grab you a few dozen."

Margo's girls slither past her into the house, yelling for Ruby as Margo backs down the porch steps and hustles to her car.

I guess I'm postponing my moping and wallowing. Isn't that the way things go? I don't even have time to feel like shit for acting like a jerk.

Ruby stomps in the back door to see what the fuss is about and her face lights up when she sees the neighbor twins. Crap, I don't even know their names...

It doesn't seem to matter, though, because Ruby takes them upstairs and I hear her door slam a few seconds later.

I sink back into the couch, taking stock of the situation. Is this babysitting? This doesn't seem too hard, comparatively. I've heard Ayana say that having more kids around the house is like having fewer kids, because they occupy each other, but it was hard for me to imagine anything like that because running out of milk is typically a category four hurricane situation. I have no wiggle room.

I lean forward with my elbows on my knees and my fists digging into my temples.

I need to make things right with Piper. I keep thinking about how she yelled about having booked vendors and prepared for her grand opening. She's right, that I could have spared her that labor at least. It was mean for me to prioritize short-term fun over reality. My reality has been a little bleak for a lot of years.

I spent a long time thinking I was only capable of joy in small snatches I could steal with my kiddo, but the past few months have really shown me so much more. And Piper was the one who catalyzed all of that. She set my life up like a speed rail, with all the pieces I need right there for me to use and build up my career and find care for my kid. I drag my hands through my hair, miserable that I fucked this all up so royally. Fricked it. No. Fucked it.

Before I can figure out what to do about this revelation, the girls flock downstairs to tell me they're hungry. "It's like ten in the morning," I mutter, not sure which meal I should be preparing at this point in the day, but since Margo mentioned eggs and milk, I decide to try my hand at French toast.

Which quickly turns out to be a failure because we don't have any syrup. Ruby glares at me. "*Piper* would have known what to do to make it taste better," she huffs. "But you chased her away."

I point a spatula at my daughter. "You walked in on the tail end of that conversation, okay, Ruby? I'm working on it."

One of the twins leans past me and sticks her head in our snack cupboard. "You have any applesauce, Ruby?"

She asks my daughter as if I'm not the authority in this house. And maybe I shouldn't be, since I clearly haven't learned how to set priorities yet. I sigh and open the cupboard further, pulling out a few squeeze pouches of applesauce that may or may not be expired.

The twin takes the pouches to the table. "We can smear this on top. Like latkes."

"What's a latke?" Thankfully, Ruby has an age-appropriate attention span, so she ditches the guilt trips temporarily for a lesson on Jewish holiday foods. I plate the toast and serve the girls, watching as they taste the combo, find it acceptable, and dig in.

I wish I had the problem-solving abilities of Margo's kid. Maybe I should ask her how to proceed with Piper.

"Hey," I start, and then remember that I don't know the girls' names. They all look up and I point at the applesauce sleuth. "Question for you. What would you do if you..." And then I freeze because I have no idea how to even summarize what I did to Piper.

Ruby frowns at me.

I look back at the kids. "Anyone know any good buildings where someone could open a gym?" I laugh because it sounds ridiculous. Children don't have their thumb on the pulse of the local real estate market.

But the twins blink at me and shrug. One twin talks with her mouth full and says, "Yeah. Dat's where our dad is. He's real torn."

"He's what?"

The applesauce kid yells, "It's real turd."

"That's what I said. He's a real turd. He sells people's houses and buildings."

I do not laugh at the mispronunciation. I scratch my

beard and reach over to pluck an uneaten piece of toast from my daughter's plate, munching contemplatively. "Does your dad know a lot about buildings?"

38

PIPER

"My head hurts." I press my cheek into the marble counters in Chloe's kitchen after staggering through her sliding glass door by the kitchen.

"You never drink that much," Chloe soothes, placing a cool, wet cloth on the back of my neck, which helps immediately. A lot. I sit up.

"Why is my voice scratchy, Chlo? Was I yelling?"

She smiles and slides me a plate of scrambled eggs with salsa. My stomach gurgles and I shove a forkful in my mouth.

"You were singing, Pipes. You were singing Celine Dion."

"Hm." I swallow the eggs. "That'll do it, I guess. Was I good?"

"You were not good." She pulls up a stool next to me and rubs my back as I eat.

Their house seems awfully quiet—no music or background sounds or dog yips. "Where is everyone?"

Chloe shrugs. "The gals all went home after you passed out. Teddy is walking T.K. We're playing soccer this morning, but you can stay as long as you want. There's no rush."

I shove in the last forkful of eggs. "I don't want to linger. Besides, I have to up my game plan. Do I remember that Juniper emailed me some stuff?"

With a nod, Chloe leans across the counter for her iPad and clicks around a few times. "It's all here in the group chat, but she thinks she has some really good case precedents for you. She's advising you to sue in small claims court, but thinks you'll get the developer to buy out your entire lease." She shows me a picture of a fierce-looking woman in a red power suit. "Soo-lin Lui. This is the lawyer she's calling for you."

"Oh, Chloe. I can't afford that. Shit. I can't even afford to sue to keep my business. Which doesn't have a physical location."

Chloe closes up the screen and pats my arm, pulling back the cloth and tossing it in the sink. "There was a discussion of a barter. Lunch break classes at the courthouse...something like that."

"I'm laughing, imagining Juniper exercising in her robe."

"Pretty sure the judges would take off the robes. But Juniper says her new chambers are large enough for a small mat class."

I sigh, standing up and walking my plate to the sink. I hang the rag over the faucet and rinse the salsa off my dishes. "That actually sounds pretty cool. I do love a good barter."

Chloe nods. "Plus, Juniper's fit as hell so I'm sure her legal friends are, too, and you can design the intense monster class of your dreams."

"All the classes are the ones of my dreams. Seriously. I love the beginner stuff almost more than the advanced level. I want to make an impact. I think I can do it."

Chloe wraps her arms around my middle. "I know you can do it. This will work out. I have to believe it."

I rest my head against hers and return the hug. "What about the stuff with Cash, though? I really liked him. Once he loosened up a little."

She pulls back and shrugs. "I'm a romance author, Piper. I have to believe that will work out, too, if it's meant to."

"Meant to." I snort. "Ugh. Anyway, thank you for the hospitality. Go kick some balls."

"Keep us posted on everything, okay?" She walks me out and I climb in my car.

I DRIVE to my house and spend about three hours in the bath tub, letting out the water and adding scalding batches periodically. Once my skin is thoroughly pruned, I stare at all the stuff Juniper sent me and then suddenly it's dark outside.

I climb into bed and, after a bunch of tossing and turning, I fall asleep. And then once I'm in bed, I can't really see a reason to get out. I'm not sure how long I spend beneath the covers before my phone starts creating a racket.

I was pretty sure I had it on vibrate, but it continues to beep and shake and eventually chirp at me, so I crawl toward it on the nightstand and then onto the floor where it falls. The chirping grows louder and more insistent, and I finally turn it around in my hand to see Samantha's face on video.

"Ah. Good. There you are."

"How are you doing this?" I squint and rub at my eyes, not entirely sure I'm awake.

"Well, I added myself to your favorites recently, and then

once your Celine concert was over, I made sure I had access to some notification settings just in case we ever needed to get in contact urgently."

I look at the phone, confused. "Urgently?"

Samantha flaps a hand. "You're in bed at ten in the morning. This is extremely unlike you. Also I'm outside. With food." She holds up a bag from the Mediterranean stand I love at the farmers market. My stomach groans.

"Okay, okay, I'm coming." I make my way to the door of my apartment and open it to find a crew of my gym clients, but no Samantha. "What the hell?" I fight to control my face, but this is all very unexpected.

Naomi pats my arm and the women walk inside. "Samantha hacked your phone for us," she says, dropping a bag of food on the table. "But we really did bring hummus!"

I walk slowly to the table and reach for a carrot, dipping it in to the fluffy, tangy goodness. I sit and eye the women warily as they, too, join me at the table. Naomi leans forward. "Look. We need you. You keep us sane, Piper. Parenthood is tough as hell."

"Really tough," Fatima echoes, snatching a carrot from the bag and dunking it emphatically in the hummus.

Naomi nods. "I know your focus is physical health stuff, but we really started to rely on your classes. Why the hell else would we be trotting around in the park with you where everyone could see?"

The women around the table all nod as they munch. I realize I'm sitting here with no bra, hair all kinds of wild, and I haven't brushed my teeth since maybe Friday. I hold my hand over my mouth in horror. Fatima sighs. "It took me a long time to get out of the fog when I had my kid. If you don't have someone hauling you up, it's just treading water, only tending to the most emergent things. I think you know that, Piper. Your classes give me that sense of being lifted up, of learning to lift myself up, too."

I start crying because her words are so powerfully meaningful. "Fatima, I love having you in my class. I love all of you." I want to hug each of them until I remember my breath once more.

Ayana pounds a fist on the table. "I know the space didn't work out for the gym. And I don't know where you're going to store all your gear and ropes and things, but we are here to tell you we'll follow you. We'll head to any park, squat on someone's porch, or hide under a bridge in the snow. We need this. Like you always say, we need to stay healthy so we can stay on this earth."

Naomi squeezes my hand. "Pipe Fitters is wherever you are, Piper. We don't care that you don't have a building right now."

I hear a deep sound, like a man clearing his throat, and I whip my head to the doorway to see Cash leaning against the frame, holding Ruby's hand. "I actually might have an idea about the building part."

As I stare in disbelief at the man in my doorway, Ayana waves at Ruby, who grins. The women all sit up straighter, stop chewing, and look to Cash, waiting.

He looks like shit, like maybe he hasn't really slept since I saw him last, or changed his clothes. Hopefully he brushed his teeth at least. I cross my arms over my chest but I don't tell him to leave. I wonder which of my students left my door hanging open, though...

Cash balls his hands into fists and then releases them. "So, my neighbor is a realtor," he starts.

"It's not turd," Ruby interjects. "It's TOR. A real TOR."

I stifle a laugh as Cash nods. "Right. Like I said, my neighbor does that job." He makes a face at Ruby, and she mimics zipping her lips together. "And Kevin was telling me about a new commercial space that's looking for tenants. Very hush-hush and new." Cash describes another former factory space just a few blocks away from my current location, only this one has already been bought by developers and fully renovated. "There's going to be a barber in there, and an art gallery. And I think a ballroom dancing classroom...anyway, they're looking for outside-the-box businesses. Their term."

Cash swallows and looks at all the women sitting around my table, really looks at them, and smiles. They smile back at him and nod. "Pipe Fitters isn't like any gym I ever tried," Fatima says.

Naomi nods. "Sounds outside the box to me!"

I eat another carrot. "Forgive me if I'm hesitant to sign another five-year lease, Cashel."

"I know. But I called Ben and he thinks this place will be more stable, since like I said, the developers already developed it."

Ayana has her phone out, tapping around, and holds up the screen with her map app. "Is this the address? Near that hippie grocery store?" Cash nods. "Mmm, we could get celery juice after we work out." Fatima and Naomi laugh. I know they're not ready for major diet changes yet, and that's okay. That's not what I focus on as a starting point. I realize I've already dipped back into work mode, thinking about my students and the changes they *can* make to improve their overall health.

I smile at Ruby and then look up at Cash. "Can I see the space?"

39

CASH

Piper's gym friends all conveniently offer to take Ruby for an extended afternoon play date once they see that Piper is interested in going with me to see the building Kevin mentioned. Ruby seems happy enough to spend the day with her friends and I am actually excited to call Kevin to let us in using his fancy realtor key codes.

"Will you ride with me?" I hung out in Piper's kitchen while she went to shower and she seemed a little relieved to see me when she emerged smelling like flowers, her damp hair tied back in a neat braid.

I did my best to splash water on my face at the sink, realizing I failed to take grooming into account when I embarked on this journey to make amends. Word gets around fast with Piper's friends, because Chloe called to tell me she heard I have "grovel hair" going on, whatever that means.

Piper bites her lip and shrugs. "I'm still mad at you."

I nod. "That's fair. But I do want to show you this place. Hell, maybe I want to rent studio space there and start actually using my garage for parking."

Piper's face brightens. "It would be so cool if you could build a more permanent booth!" I hadn't even really given thought to renting space for my voice work, but Chloe says she has a lot of work for me if I want it. And the money is right.

If I can just get Piper to forgive me, I might say everything is going my way.

I gesture toward the door and we walk out to my car, Piper wondering aloud how a recording studio might live harmoniously in the same building where she intends to blast her music and hurl weights around.

"Maybe I should just waterproof my basement and stick closer to home."

She snorts, and then gets quiet as I drive back toward my neighborhood. "I just wish you'd said something to me, Cash. I'm the most mad at being in a position for Ben to shock me. I cried in front of him."

I groan as I slow to a stop at a red light. "I hear you and you're right. All I can say is I *was* being selfish in that moment. I was looking short-term at a nice week with you when I could have been building your trust, working alongside you on a solution and, I don't know...planning for a nice *life* with you, Piper."

She crosses her arms over her chest protectively. "Well... that's a really nice thing for you to say." I turn and give her a grin before flicking on my turn signal and parking at the former warehouse.

Kevin waves from the doorway and I hurry around the front of the car to open Piper's door for her. I want to put my arm around her as we walk toward the building, but I'm not sure I'm back in that layer of her good graces just yet.

From where I'm standing, the building looks just like the

previous Pipe Fitters, but with modern electricity and fewer holes in the wall. But Piper seems delighted. "I love the high ceilings," she coos. "And there's already fans up there, so we won't stink up the joint as much!"

Kevin laughs and they continue walking around. "So," he says, pausing, "I understand your finances are in purgatory for a bit, but we can look at paperwork on Monday if you want. There are some grant opportunities I think the owner would recommend for you."

"Grants?" Piper's eyes fly wide and she halts.

Kevin nods. "Oh yeah. The developer is really looking to push women-owned businesses, especially those with a mission to support women in the community. There are a few different funding streams that might work based on what Cash said you do here."

She arches a brow and turns to look at me. "Oh yeah? What did he say we do, exactly?"

Kevin scratches his chin and seems nervous. I shrug, and he says, "Well, you focus on women, mothers in particular, and introduce sustainable movement into their lives to improve cardiovascular health. I think that's the part that piqued my interest, because there's a specific grant about healthy communities." Kevin hands Piper a brochure and her eyes well up as she looks over the information.

"This is amazing. This is just what I had in mind. I encourage my clients to keep up with well-woman care, too. I would love to help this study about diabetes risk factors..."

Kevin smiles and slides a business card into her hand along with the brochure. "Cash has my number, but here's my card. This isn't in the MLS yet—appointments are word of mouth right now. Let's talk soon, okay? We can get you up and running."

He walks us out and waves as he hops into his car, probably to get back home to Margo and the girls. Which leaves me alone with Piper, leaning against my car and staring at the papers in her hands.

"Cash, I don't know what to say."

I risk sidling up a little closer to her. "Say you forgive me?"

She nudges me with her shoulder. "I'll work on it for sure." She bites her lip. "How do you know Kevin? Who even are you? These grant programs paired with the small claims settlement can really get me helping more women, quickly..."

I scratch my beard and stare at the traffic passing by. "I realized I need to pull my chin up and talk to people. Some loud woman in lycra got me to rely on other people, and then it turns out people have good ideas."

"Some loud woman, hm?" Piper turns so she's facing me directly, her body an inch from mine. "What makes this woman loud?"

I grin and lean closer, daring to invade her space. My chest brushes against hers and I meet her eyes, which twinkle joyfully, so I inch closer. "She's loudest when I lick her," I whisper, and Piper tugs me by the hair, pressing our mouths together.

We kiss breathlessly until I can't take it anymore and I wrench her door open. "Sit tight," I growl, jumping in the car and roaring toward my house as she laughs.

She holds my hand as I rush toward the front door, ignoring the neighbors who are out in their front yards, waving at me. Piper of course waves at all the kids running around, but I tug her inside and slam the door. "I have my whole life to work on being social," I tell her, dropping to my knees in front of her, pressing her back against the door. "Right now I just want to make you scream."

Piper nods and I pull down her pants, kissing and licking her thighs in the process. She kicks off her sneakers and I strip her bare, spreading her legs apart with my hands and licking her naval. That wonderful taut skin of hers quivers at my touch and I feel so grateful to be here, worshipping at the feet of the person who showed me it's okay for me to reach for things. Who helped me find a network of other people to give me a boost.

"Cash, that feels good. Oh!" She cries out as I nip at the sensitive skin on her upper thighs and then slide a thumb along her seam. She groans as I explore, pressing against her clit in the way she showed me last time. And this time I can savor her pleasure, watch her in broad daylight as I get to be the one to make her feel good.

"I...want...bed..." Piper pants and bangs her head off the front door as I slide my fingers in and out of her warmth and lap at her with my tongue.

"In a minute," I say, tossing one of her legs over my shoulder and hooking my arm under her thigh to support her weight. From this angle, I can stroke her with all four fingers and rest my cheek against her other leg. I feel the powerful muscles vibrating and I know she's close. And I know that takes some effort, so I let myself enjoy this moment right alongside her as she comes, screaming my name, hands flailing in my hair, pinching at my ears.

"I love doing that for you," I whisper, kissing her inner thigh as she calms down. When Piper starts to sink toward the floor, I scoop her up and stagger upstairs, trying not to bash her knees off the wall or hit the bannister with her head.

She laughs when I toss her on my bed, and then she pounces so she's straddling me, and I get my favorite view in the universe when she strips off her shirt and leans over to bring her nipples close to my mouth. "Take your clothes off, Cashel," she commands, and I don't make her ask twice. As I struggle out of my shirt and sweats, she rummages in the night stand, exclaiming cheerfully when she finds the carton of condoms I grabbed from the store before I fucked up our relationship progress.

I laugh as she whips me with one of the strips, but things get serious real fast when she tears off a packet, rips it open, and rolls it along my length. I watch in awe as she lines herself up and sinks down onto me, her face melting into pleasure again as I fill her. I can't believe I get to share this moment, that I get to experience this raw vulnerability and see Piper simultaneously strong and tender.

I wrap my hands around her hips, feeling the warmth of her as she moves, and I pull myself up to press my chest against her, easing my tongue into her mouth and tasting each one of her moans. "I want this with you, Piper," I mutter.

"You've got it, Cash." Her breath comes fast and hot against my cheek.

I realize now that I love this so much because I've seen all of her—the joy and the sorrow, the struggle and the success. The intimacy is deeper because I was part of a solution, alongside her for a challenge instead of suffering alone. "I want you," I tell her, punctuating my words with kisses. "All of you. Every part."

"Yes," she says, and drops her head back. I slide a hand between us, thrusting up into her faster until I feel my own barriers explode. She wraps her legs around me and digs her nails into my shoulders and I feel her pulsing around me. Piper starts to come, and I topple over the edge with her, groaning her name as I pour myself into her.

I tip over backwards and she lets me pull her with me, the two of us sweating and clinging together like two pieces of a braid. It's uncomfortable and perfect all at once.

40

PIPER

EVEN THOUGH IT'LL BE AT LEAST THREE MONTHS UNTIL I CAN officially start my lease, Kevin hooked me up with a per diem rate for the large event space in my new building, and I was able to resume Pipe Fitters classes immediately.

I have more students than ever filing in to jump rope and squat our butts off. I even have some of my advanced students carrying weight equipment from the first space to the new one in relay teams.

I spend a lot of my down time at Cash and Ruby's house, especially on days Ruby has a half-day from school. She was delighted to learn Cash and I are "boyfriend-girlfriend" and I keep waiting for things to get awkward, but it just doesn't happen.

Today, I wait with Margo and Toi for the school bus while Cash finishes a last-minute call to install a home charging port for an electric vehicle. Teddy actually got him thinking about offering that, and had Cash install some gadgets at the cottage for Chloe's Tesla.

Cash grumbled about having to order new tools for the

job, but I can tell he's excited for his family business to be able to offer a new service. Cash wants his dad to hire a full-time electrician so Cash can stay on part-time, and leave room in his schedule for audiobook narration now that word is getting out about his performance for Chloe.

RUBY BOUNDS out of the bus and into my arms and I relish the feel of her little cheek against mine as we hug. "I can never get enough hugs," I explain. I wave to Margo and Toi as we head toward the Brennan pad.

"Why don't you have enough hugs?" Ruby shakes her hand around instead of asking for the keys, and I know she likes to be the one to unlock the door, so I let her have the whole bundle.

"Well," I explain, "My mom died when I was a kid. My dad was never much of a hugger."

"Hmm." Ruby holds up a key, glancing at me for approval and I nod because she found the right one. "My mom's dead, too. But Cash says we can find lots of people to love us."

"That's true. I like hugging *you.*"

She shoves open the door. "And you like hugging my dad."

"I do. He's very fuzzy. Like a sweater."

Ruby drops her bag on the ground and I bite my lip. "Hey, Rubes, can you put the bag on the hook? Your dad said that's a rule."

She pouts and stares at it. I hang my own purse on a hook and she sighs, picking up her backpack, too. "Can we swing the hammer at the tires?"

I shake my head. "Homework first."

Ruby pouts. "It was more fun when we were in the gym."

"Yeah, it was fun there, but once you do your homework we can make pepperoni rolls again! I got some strawberries to have with dinner."

This seems to appease her and I enjoy working through some math before we use the same types of problems as we break up the dough and add pepperonis and cheese. Cash arrives home just as I slide the roll into the oven and I squeal when he hugs Ruby and I together with a growl before kissing us each on the forehead.

We share a pleasant meal together as he explains the growing demand for electric vehicle charging stations, but I start to grow antsy after we all help wash and put away the dishes. "I have to get some stuff done for Pipe Fitters 2.0," I tell him, my gaze drifting toward my bag and the front door.

"Can you work on it here?" Cash raises a brow and shoos Ruby into the living room, where she quickly proceeds to turn on her music and dance.

"What would that look like?" He steps closer to me and wraps his arms around me in a hug that might look perfectly acceptable to passersby, but flips my stomach upside down and sends pulsing waves to my core.

"Well," he nibbles my ear. "I could put Ruby to bed while you work. And then I could sit next to you on the couch and read the manuscript I just got from Chloe's author friend."

"That sounds nice." I lean into his hug, tracing my finger along the name tag on his work shirt that he's still wearing.

"Mmm hmm. Then..." He leans close and whispers directly into my ear. "We could act out what I read in the book..."

I gasp and my hips rock toward his involuntarily, but I place my palm on his chest, because we still have to figure out the logistics of this thing before we wind up in a snarl again. "But then what? Do I have to drive home all... exhausted after?"

Cash pulls back a little, considering. He runs his fingers through his beard. "Hey, Rubes?"

"What? I'm dancing!"

Cash walks into the living room and turns down the music. She crosses her arms and looks so much like him that I giggle.

"Ruby, what would you think if Piper had a sleepover?"

"On a school night?" Ruby looks horrified, which is fair because I've seen Cash say no to such things a number of times just over the past few days.

Cash nods. "Piper works really early in the morning, anyway. You know about her exercise classes."

Ruby seems to ponder this for a minute and then shrugs. "Can she braid my hair in the princess crown again?"

"Yes," I tell her. "Definitely."

Ruby gives her dad a thumbs up and then turns the music back up. I smile at Cash. "I'm not really prepared for a sleepover tonight, though. I don't have any of my stuff..."

It's his turn to shrug and he starts to dance with Ruby. "Go get some stuff. Bring a box of stuff."

"Yeah?"

He grins. "I'm about to have an entire garage worth of storage space. Bring a steamer trunk."

I laugh and join in the dancing. "Only old timey people say things like steamer trunk."

"Is that so? I'm reading an old timey book. Maybe you've heard of it? I could read some out loud..."

I flush and Ruby shuts off the music abruptly. "I want you to read. Can we read about steamer trunks?"

I cackle and walk toward the door, leaving Cash to talk his way out of this scenario. I dash to my apartment and grab a bag full of clothes, eager to get back for my very own bedtime story.

EPILOGUE: PIPER
THREE MONTHS LATER

"Ayana, thank you so much for keeping Ruby this weekend. We will take Emerald next time so you and Geron can go out."

Ayana grins as Ruby piles into the back of the car next to Emerald. "Oh, so it's 'we' now, is it?"

I flush and shrug, adjusting the straps on my jumpsuit. "Yeah. It's we. Or, it will be if he ever gets his butt out here so we can leave. Cash!"

I holler in the front door for the man of the hour. A few weeks ago, we had a very different sort of celebration for the grand re-re-opening of Pipe Fitters, where everyone wore workout gear and families used the on-site drop in childcare available to all tenants and clients using the building. Ruby loves hanging out with all the kids whose parents are in the barber shop or make-your-own candle store or any of the other dozen small businesses inside.

Tonight, we're off to Bridges and Bitters for Chloe's book release party, where Cash Brennan is supposed to give a reading for fans of the audiobook. "Cash!" Ayana joins me shouting up the stairs and we hear him grumble and stomp down the steps.

Both of us gasp when we see him, hair and beard neatly trimmed, wearing the hell out of a tailored gray suit and new shoes. "I'm uncomfortable."

He tugs at his neck and looks like he's about to yank off his tie and I gasp. "Don't you dare!" I rush to his side and grip his lapels, looking hungrily into his eyes. "You look amazing. Utterly breathtaking."

He grunts and then looks at me in my sparkly jumpsuit and heels. "You look beautiful."

Ayana claps her hands. "You're both gorgeous." She blows us kisses and the girls wave from the back seat of the car. "Send me a picture. No. Don't. I'm taking one and then I don't want you to think about the kids all night." She snaps a quick photo and waves again. "Enjoy!"

CASH DRIVES his new electric sedan, despite my protests that we could find better parking in my tiny Fiat. "I've got this," he growls, waving past the valet Samantha seems to have procured for the evening. Cash slips the car into a spot a block down from the bar, sliding his arm behind my seat for the backing up portion of the parallel park, in a move that still gives me as big a rush as the first time.

Hand in hand, we enter the bar to a flurry of applause and squeals as all the women of Foof and their partners raise a glass. I smile until my face hurts as I cling to Cash's arm, watching him slowly relax and accept the positive attention.

I tug his arm and lead him to the bar, eager to see what Esther has prepared for this special night. We duck and dodge past tables heaped with signed copies of the paper-back and I wave to get Esther's attention. She sidles over to us with a smile. "Ready for a Scofflaw?"

I laugh. "Is that related to the book? I haven't even gotten to read it yet." I jab Cash in the ribs with my elbow. "Someone says I have to wait and let him perform it for me one chapter at a time."

Esther rolls her eyes. "That's gross but it makes you happy so I'll allow it. But yes, based on Chloe's plot summary I made the Scofflaw—rye whiskey from a local distillery, dry vermouth, lemon juice, Grenadine, orange zest." She slides us glasses of the lovely dark liquid and pops a twist on the rim.

Cash and I clink glasses and sip. "Oooh, that's nice." He nods.

Esther pats the bar. "Enjoy, kids. It's nuts here." And she's off to serve a throng of bock lovers.

I lean against Cash, sipping my drink and enjoying the dance of his fingers along my waist. But I soon realize he's breathing awkwardly and emitting discomfort. "What's up?"

He shrugs. "I don't like all this."

I sigh and pat his chest. "Of course you don't. It's tons of happy people being noisy and carefree." He doesn't laugh at my joke and I set my drink on the bar. "What would help you relax?"

Cash frowns and then raises an eyebrow. My chin drops. "You can't be serious."

He downs the rest of his drink and makes a face at me that implies everything filthy and daring all at once. I suck in a breath and look around, trying to think where we might run off without drawing too much attention. "There's a closet by Esther's office," I whisper, and he squeezes my hand.

"Show me."

I nod my head as subtly as I can and start walking down the hall, past the party room where we meet for Foof. Past the bathrooms and past Esther's office. Cash is close behind me, and he whisks me into the closet, yanking the chain to turn on the light just as he slams the door shut behind us. His mouth is on me, urgently, in a flash and he lifts me up to sit on a case of something that clinks and tinkles as we jostle the crate.

"How the hell do you get this thing off?" Cash runs his hands up and down my sides, looking for an access point in my outfit and I grin at him, reach up for the neck and untying the strings until my breasts tumble free from the shimmery material.

With a groan he rips open the fly of his pants as I wriggle the waist down. We don't need much room, and it doesn't take long until he's inside me, my knees splayed open and my ankles tangled in the fabric of my jumpsuit. "I love being here with you," he whispers into my ear, sliding into me with deep, slow strokes.

"This is a party for you," I pant, bracing myself on the edge of the crate, feeling like I might combust under the heat of his gaze.

"*This* is the party I want." Cash sucks on my neck briefly and pulls back, staring at me, stilling his hips. "You're everything I want, Piper."

I melt a little more each time he tells me that and I scooch forward on the crate until I can reach him. I pull him closer to me by the tie, pressing his lips to mine and urging him to move again inside me. "I love you, Cashel Brennan, you old grump."

"I love you, too."

It's not the first time we exchanged these words, and it

won't be the last, but each time feels special, colossal. We worked so hard to get here, together, to reach this point of our lives professionally and interpersonally. Cash thrusts a few more times and I feel the tingle of impending release. I grab for his hand, yanking it in between our bodies where the snarl of zippers and fabric doesn't impede him from finding my clit.

He claps his other hand over my mouth as I moan and come around him and he grins before pressing his forehead against mine and coming inside me with a shudder and a low groan. We catch our breath and laugh at the absurdity of our situation. Backing up slightly, Cash spies a case of bar napkins and grabs a wad of them to help me clean up.

A FEW MINUTES LATER, tucked in with hair patted back into place, we pull open the door to the closet and are startled to see a man standing on the other side of the door, tan-skinned hand raised to turn the knob himself.

"Can we help you?" I peer around Cash's shoulder, unused to seeing anyone outside of Foof back in this part of the bar.

"I'm looking for the owner," he says with a smile, his accent thick and unfamiliar to me.

"What do you need with Esther?" I put my hands on my hips as Cash shakes his head and points toward the front, about to tell the man where to find her.

He grins and slides his hands in his pockets. "Gotta catch up with my wife," he says, and walks away, leaving Cash and me alone in the hall.

"Did he say wife?" I fiddle with Cash's collar, not sure what to make of this latest development.

Cash shrugs. "Who knows. We might be drunk on sex or Scofflaws, or both."

"Hm." I sigh and smile as I hear the sound of Samantha speaking into a microphone.

"Can we get a round of applause for Chloe and Cash for the production of this amazing piece of literature?" The room erupts into cheers and applause.

"Come on, Cash-quatch." I grin and give him a shove down the hall. "Your fans await."

THANK you for reading Speed Rail! I hope you loved this single dad romance. Esther's book is Last Call: A Marriage of Convenience Romance. You don't want to miss this marriage of convenience romance.

Want more Piper and Cash? My newsletter subscribers get a steamy bonus scene.

If you're new to the series, check out Fireball: An Enemies to Lovers Romance for a first glimpse into the world of Bridges and Bitters.

ALSO BY LAINEY DAVIS

Sappy Go Lucky (Eva and Asher)

Since You've Bean Gone (Ethan and Lia) *part of the Farm 2 Forking series

Brady Family Series

Foundation: A Grouchy Geek Romance (Zack and Nicole)

Suspension: An Opposites Attract Romance (Liam and Maddie)

Inspection: A Silver Fox Romance (Kellen and Elizabeth)

Vibration: An Accidental Roommates Romance (Cal and Logan)

Current: A Secret Baby Romance (Orla and Walt)

Restoration: A Silver Fox Redemption Romance (Mick and Celeste)

Oak Creek Series

The Nerd and the Neighbor (Hunter and Abigail)

The Botanist and the Billionaire (Diana and Asa)

The Midwife and the Money (Archer and Opal)

The Planner and the Player (Fletcher and Thistle)

Stone Creek University

Deep in the Pocket: A Football Romance

Hard Edge: A Hockey Romance

Possession: A Football Romance